What the critics are saying...

"FIREWALKERS: DREAMER is an enjoyable paranormal, erotic romance with an interesting premise. I found myself fascinated by Ms. Walker's world..." ~ *Marlene Breakfield, Paranormal Romance Reviews*

"Shiloh Walker has created another story that won't soon be forgotten. If you love erotic vampire tales of adventure, then pick up this book as soon as possible." ~ *Angel Brewer, just Erotic Romance Reviews*

"This reviewer found herself captured from the first page to the last, and let me tell you... I did not want it to end." ~ *Teri, Fallen Angel Reviews*

Dreamer

Firewalkers

Shiloh Walker

FIREWALKERS: DREAMER
An Ellora's Cave Publication, March 2005

Ellora's Cave Publishing, Inc.
1337 Commerce Drive, Suite #13
Stow, Ohio 44224

ISBN #1419951599

Edited by: *Pamela Campbell*
Cover art by: Syneca

Warning:

The following material contains graphic sexual content meant for mature readers. *Firewalkers: Dreamer* has been rated *E-rotic* by a minimum of three independent reviewers.

Ellora's Cave Publishing offers three levels of Romantica™ reading entertainment: S (S-ensuous), E (E-rotic), and X (X-treme).

S-*ensuous* love scenes are explicit and leave nothing to the imagination.

E-*rotic* love scenes are explicit, leave nothing to the imagination, and are high in volume per the overall word count. In addition, some E-rated titles might contain fantasy material that some readers find objectionable, such as bondage, submission, same sex encounters, forced seductions, etc. E-rated titles are the most graphic titles we carry; it is common, for instance, for an author to use words such as "fucking", "cock", "pussy", etc., within their work of literature.

X-*treme* titles differ from E-rated titles only in plot premise and storyline execution. Unlike E-rated titles, stories designated with the letter X tend to contain controversial subject matter not for the faint of heart.

Dreamer
Firewalker

Dedication

This one is for Anni and Renee! I love ya, ladies!

And to Jerry...always to Jerry...my life just wouldn't be complete without you.

Hugs to my babies!

Prologue
2338 A.D.

It was only about ten p.m. American Eastern Standard Time when it happened. The United Federal States of America, which now consisted of America, Mexico, a number of the smaller islands in the tropics and many of the small Central American countries was settling down after yet another prosperous day. It looked like they would be drawing Canada into the Government before much time passed.

It was good times for America. The past century had been good.

A young woman was crossing the tiny, well-kept lawn of her home after walking her licensed pet, requisite waste receptacle in hand, when she heard and felt an odd rushing noise. The flutter in her womb caused her to lay a protective hand on her belly. She looked up absently, and found she could not look away.

The sky was red.

Brilliant, ruby-red.

Some thought it was the end of the world.

Less than a third of the population believed in the being called God. Those people flocked to churches and synagogues and prayed.

Scientists were in a flurry of movement all over the world. The bizarre phenomenon had been going on for more than three days now. The sky was nearly blood-red at night, and tinged purple, almost lilac during the day.

Other, less religious, less logical thinkers, thought there were beings from outer space coming. There had been several encounters with other races by now, but for the most part, the races Earth people had met had not wanted much to do with them.

And over the past several decades, the people from Earth had been slowly becoming more Earthbound. Fascination with space travel had faded. The rather fantastic space stations were abandoned and the space ports that had once called out to the rich and famous were now desolate. There was even talk of NASA being disbanded.

The talk about creatures from outer space had died rather quickly—because more fantastic things had occurred. The red haze had started to coalesce over the eastern borders of the United Federal States of America, and people all over the world saw the normal nighttime sky for the first time in three days. But the people of America, particularly New York, Boston, and Washington, looked out their windows and saw red. It wasn't possible that people from cities all up and down the east coast could see it at the same time, but it was happening.

It towered into the air, human shaped, with arms and legs, shoulders and a torso, a head with streaming ribbons of fiery red. It looked like a man made of fire. The formation process took more than two days, and as is natural with men, they became more and more frightened.

Fear mounted. But the thing seemed to be illusion or mist or vapor. Nothing that was done to it seemed to have any effect.

It responded to no voice, no threat, no promise.

It responded to none of the firepower, none of the gases, nothing.

And on the seventh day after the red mist first settled over the planet, the being started to walk, from the east coast to the west. The journey across the country took the man/demon/God seven days. With each day, it dissipated, little pieces of the creature fluttering down here and there, like red glitter, fading away into the night. By the time it reached the new beaches that had been formed when California had fallen into the sea after the massive earthquakes of 2241, it was all but gone.

The red fires reformed, though, until the men with cameras who had been following had to turn their heads away from the brightness. It coalesced again, brighter and brighter, and then it exploded. With a mighty roar, the first sound it had made, the man made of fire was gone.

The effects from the creature were not seen in that generation.

Nor in the next.

It wasn't until children were born to the children who had been conceived around the time that the demon fell to earth that odd things were noticed. Children born with gifts, or curses, depending on how you looked at it. A few cropped up in Europe—fewer still in the Middle East, which was in truth a blessing.

The few gifted who were discovered there were not just killed, they were tortured to death, while the people cheered and watched.

A handful from Asia and other eastern countries. A rather startling number from Australia and New Zealand.

But the United Federal States…they were nearly overwhelmed. Children were talking at six months. A telepath was discovered when she was 12 months old. A four-year-old fire starter was nearly put to death but some brave soul smuggled the frightened child out of the state before the government could follow through. Parents started to hide the gifted children.

But other parents started to kill their own blood.

An underground movement formed. Nurses were trained to recognize the gifted children, born with eyes that glowed in just the right light, if one knew what to look for. They were taken from the hospital and spirited away before their own parents could harm them.

Some called them the demon touched.

But others knew the creature hadn't fallen from space, or been sent from Hell.

The man of fire had been a gift, or a last warning.

Too many things were going wrong. He was sent to give them peacekeepers—the children who were being killed in their cribs. They were to be the protectors, the enforcers, one last attempt to save a fallen world.

They called themselves the Firewalkers.

Chapter One
The Dreamer

Caris left the computer and stretched her arms high overhead. Her head ached and felt tight, so she pulled the band from her honey blonde hair, letting the heavy, straight locks fall free down her back as she left the silence of her room.

Another child had been captured, but one of her kind had saved the boy. Anger stiffened her body as she paced the spacious log home nestled in the foothills of Montana. Her parents had left her acres and acres of land. The land alone made her a rich woman, but she needed it...needed to be there.

Two of her gifts were telepathy and empathy. If she spent too much time around others, their emotions and thoughts would slowly drive her mad. She knew how to shield, but she could not constantly do it. She had to leave herself open and listen for those who were preying on the Firewalkers, especially the children.

In the twenty-five years since her birth, the government had developed more advanced ways of searching and the Firewalkers needed all the resources they could muster. Thank God for men like Sage. Sage Monroe was a thought sensor, but a selective one. He only seemed to home in on thoughts of those in need, and he was also a teleporter. He was one of their most valuable assets.

But that particular agent was a walking time bomb.

His rage was a palpable thing. Too many more near misses like today's, and he was going to sacrifice himself just to kill the men who threatened the helpless children he was saving.

The Firewalkers were doing everything they could. But it was not enough.

Every day, one of the captured children died. Every day, more and more of the Firewalkers were sacrificed in the fight to save the youngest of their brethren.

"Stop it," Caris whispered harshly to herself as tears threatened.

Sliding into a pit of depression would do nothing to save the lost. Would do nothing to protect the vulnerable.

The simple cotton shirt that she wore over her slim golden body did little to hide her lithe muscular form. Long legs, left bare, were strong and taut thanks to the hours she spent riding her horses over her land. And her hands were deadly—although if she ever had to use any of the dirtier tricks Sage had taught her in a fight to the death, she'd probably go mad.

You couldn't fight without touching, couldn't kill a person without touching them.

But she'd had to force herself to learn.

If it came down to a choice of kill or be killed...she'd risk the madness.

Her long, thick golden locks lay heavily on her shoulders, streaming behind her as she paced in quick, long strides, her agitation written all over her heart-shaped face, her golden eyes sparking with it.

She realized she was leaking, spilling emotion all over, and forced herself to stop, to breathe, to relax.

Sighing, Caris settled down in the basement across from Erik and his borrowed body with a gentle, reassuring smile on her face as Miguel keyed the laz-lock on the shelter open.

The intruder spat out, "Get away from me, you filthy diseased fuck-freak."

Miguel just laughed and flicked a hand toward him. "That's a funny one, *amigo*. Now be nice. Don't make me remember I don't like you. And before I decide to wrap that mouth shut. I have company for you."

Sometime later, she had fallen asleep, a hungry sigh on her lips, sliding her fingers inside her panties. The vampire in the story had made her hunger and wish — she shouldn't have read it right now. Aching and wishing were not good things for Caris. Odd things tended to happen when she was needy, wishing, and weak.

While sleeping, her fingers grazed the hard nub of her clit. In her dream, it was a vampire lover, with deep, deep chestnut hair, shot through with thick strands of red. His face was leonine, tawny gold, handsome, his mouth clever and sexy, a full lower lip, a thin, sensual upper one. Right now, that mouth was on her belly, sliding down further, and then he was feeding from her, his fangs piercing the vein in her thigh as he thrust two long fingers deep inside her.

Her vampire — she waited for him, constantly. Yearned for him. She wanted him here. She sobbed in her sleep, drove her fingers inside her slippery sheath, and climaxed, while yearning for the sweet pain of a bite, the heavy weight of a man's body on hers, the pleasure of joining her mind with another's, of finding somebody like her.

In her heart, she thought he was real. He felt real. In her head, she knew vampires didn't exist.

Damn it, you're supposed to be here. Come and find me!

Then she settled into true sleep, unaware of what her mind and her powers had been doing while she was dreaming.

Chapter Two
The Vampire

Damn the bitch to the lowest level of Hell, Jax thought viciously. The Princess Kyrel had arranged for her Guard to kidnap him. Then she had starved him. Once the Bloodlust had nearly driven him insane, she locked herself into the room with him and removed the heavy verstael restraints.

He stalked away from her.

"I've no desire to fuck you, or to have my head cut from my body, Princess. Leave me be," he snarled at her.

She laughed. "If you had fucked me the first time, it wouldn't have come to this, Jax. All I wanted was to have the sexy vampire as my lover."

"As your lapdog," he spat, trying to ignore the scent of her blood.

She smiled, her red lips curving as she drew a slim knife from the belt at her hip. "All one and the same," she purred as she took the knife and cut a tiny nick in her throat.

Jax watched her with morbid fascination as the trickle of blood flowed enticingly down her pale neck.

His fangs dropped, his cock swelled. He couldn't fight the fucking blood hunger. "I've no desire to sink my dick inside you," he rasped, lisping a bit around his fangs. "Your pussy probably has teeth."

Her eyes narrowed. Then she rubbed a finger in the blood while she unzipped her black flight suit. It clung like a second skin and she wore nothing under it.

The Princess Kyrel was a bloody whore. All but her father knew it. No wonder he couldn't arrange an honorable match for her.

But Jax was not about to point that out to King Morain. Morain was a decent and kind man. He was simply blind where Kyrel was concerned. He fought off the need to growl and fall on her like an animal as she painted her nipple with her own blood. "Stop it," he rasped. "I'm near starving, Princess. If I feed, I fuck. And you're in heat. If I father a child on you, both I and the child are put to death. Are you so fucking cruel that you would sacrifice two people just to get laid?"

She laughed as she gathered more blood and started to paint a trail down her slim belly. "I do not care who pays, so long as I get to fuck you, Jax. If you had let me take my pleasure when first I commanded it, it would not have come to this."

The hunger was closing in and he could not fight it.

He lunged for her, taking her down and closing his mouth over the tiny wound. Her blood was flat, metallic, rather surprising. The blood of a royal was usually a fine wine, and with her being ripe—ah well, it was blood and he needed it.

He wanted to bellow out with rage as her fingers found the tab to his flight pants and opened them. Her hand closed over his cock and he knocked it aside as he fed. She called for her guards, and he fought as they pinned him.

It took seven of them, but he was weak from nearly two weeks without feeding. Two on each leg, one at each arm and another at his head held him as she straddled him, pulled her neck from him, and sank down on his rigid cock. "See," she purred as she rode him. "I knew you wanted me."

He glared up at her, fought the urge to spit. "I do not want you, Princess. A male vampire's cock gets hard when he feeds. I've fed from animals before and it's gotten hard. And I'd rather have fucked one of those animals than you," he said coldly. He closed his eyes and ordered himself not to struggle. Not to come.

He was pleasantly surprised to discover it wasn't that hard.

Though his cock ached, and his balls ached, he didn't want the Princess, and he never had. Jax suspected he could keep it up for a week if that's what it took to keep an unwanted half-breed child from being put to death.

He forced himself into a meditative state, the half slumber that took over his kind when the sun rose in the sky, the lighter slumber that preceded the deep, nearly catatonic sleep.

Jax was dimly aware of the slippery, loose grasp of her pussy on his cock, but unmoved by it. He could smell other men on her, mostly her guards, chemicals and tobacco. "You reek, Princess," he said, biting his cheek to keep from laughing when she hissed at him in rage. His head hit the floor as one of her guards struck him in the face.

He didn't retaliate. He could have. Tasteless as her blood was, he felt better. She drove herself harder down on him and commanded, "Look at me."

He opened his eyes and stared up at her, his blue gaze cold and blank. "Does your father know you enjoy raping his men, Kyrel?" he asked.

She gasped in shock and slammed herself down. "Your dick is hard. You want me. This is not rape."

"It is hard because I am vampire. We associate feeding with fucking. I cannot help that, but I do not want you," he said. "If I had wanted you, I would have shot you full of seed the minute I was buried inside you, after being forced to go two weeks without sex. If I had wanted you, I would have already come. You can keep riding me with your used little body until the sun rises and I will still not come. I am unwilling—I do not want to be held down by seven armed men while you ride me." He grunted as her nails raked his face in her rage and she started to thrust harder and harder until he knew she was hurting herself.

"You will make yourself sore," he taunted her. "And I am vampire, not human, so while your flesh is chafed and raw, I will not suffer at all."

"Silence," one of the guards growled. "Or do you want me to cut out your fucking tongue?"

He grinned insolently. "The King is already asking for me. I'm one of his more valued hunters. Do you really think you can get by with that?"

"When I tell him I saw you abusing his daughter? Yes," the guard spat.

"I'll insist on Truth Judgment. Even the Princess Kyrel cannot deny me, a lowly vampire, that," he said. Then he closed his eyes and retreated, fighting the urge to laugh at the ridiculous situation. Kyrel screamed in rage and threw herself off of him and into the arms of one of her guards.

"Hurt him," she sobbed as she pulled the guard eagerly into her arms.

And they did.

Only sunlight or beheading would kill him.

But a beating most certainly hurt.

* * * * *

Jax moved slowly into the chamber before King Morain and dropped to both knees. It hurt viciously to do so, but he refused to show it. He was here to try and save his life. The Princess wasn't pregnant, because he had never come inside her, but she had claimed he had fed from her without her consent and raped her.

The King himself would oversee this hearing, and Jax was humbled by such trust. If the King hadn't truly believed in Jax, he would have been turned over to a lesser court, and probably been given less fair treatment. Though they couldn't have denied him Truth Judgment, even he knew how easy it would be for a small contingent of men loyal to the Princess to come upon him unaware, while he slept. How easy for them to cast his unprotected body in the sun — charring his flesh, fiery flames eating at him even before he was completely aware. All too easy.

But if the King himself presided, none would dare touch Jax without the King's express orders.

"The Princess Kyrel claims you fed without consent and raped her," Morain said without preamble. There was only him and two others in the room.

Jax had refused counsel. He didn't trust anybody besides himself, the King, and Faraman — who wasn't in the galaxy — more's the pity. "I beg your apology, and your permission to speak frankly, my Lord King," Jax said without lifting his eyes.

Morain sighed. "Stand up, Jax." His eyes narrowed as the tall, powerful vampire moved slowly and painfully. "Why are you moving so oddly?"

Jax remained silent, one hand wrapped around a thick wrist, keeping himself from driving his hands through his hair, or punching a wall. The rage that filled him would do him no good here.

"I asked you a question. Consider it an order that you answer, old friend," Morain said softly, his eyes holding a warning.

Jax stared briefly into the king's eyes before he released the tabs on his flight jacket, revealing the healing bruises and myriad injuries on his torso. Morain's mouth tightened. A vampire's anatomy was a wonderful thing— they healed quickly. The beating Jax took would be gone in less than a week, if Morain was judging correctly. But that also meant that if a human had taken such a beating, he'd be dead. The burns would have been third degree, Morain was thinking, the bruises deep and to the bone. Most likely, there were a number of bones broken that had already healed.

"Who dared to harm one of my men so?" Morain asked in a calm, quiet voice that did little to conceal his rage.

Without blinking an eye, Jax repeated, "I beg permission to speak frankly."

"Bloody hell, Jax. You're no serf or pauper or slave in my kingdom. You are welcome to speak as you choose," Morain said.

Jax blinked once, slowly. His long lashes slid down to cover his sapphire-blue eyes before he said softly, "I must beg permission before I am allowed to take a wife. I will never be allowed to father a child. You tried to geld me when I was twenty—you may not make me wear a slave collar, but I hardly feel free."

"Jax," Morain sighed. "You know why. Your kind are too strong. And most are not as you are. You are honorable. Bloody hell, I know you did not rape Kyrel. You are a man of honor, of decency, of valor. But you are easily ten times stronger than my strongest soldier. You will live to be at least a thousand years old, and you are only fifty. You can control minds, you can sense thoughts and fears. Your intelligence alone is a weapon. You speak more than fifty languages, and will learn ten times that, with your psychic gifts. Hell, all you have to do is touch a person, and you have their tongue.

"The world was once dominated by the vampires. I fear vampires could very well take over the galaxy. We cannot allow it to ever happen again. We were the slaves once."

"So because of that, now I am to be the slave," Jax said softly. He closed his eyes and held up his hand. "Enough. This is not why we are here. No, my Lord, I did not rape your daughter. I highly doubt such an act against her is possible. Four months ago, she started pursuing me and I refused her. I beg your pardon, my Lord, but the woman is relentless. I have found her everywhere, in my lodging, aboard my ship, at the way station on Creor Nine.

"Two weeks ago, when my yearly leave began, I was returning to my lodging in Veral when her men overtook me. They drugged me with cerpsyllium, bound me with verstael restraints and I woke in her chambers in this very castle. If you send some of the vampire hunters, they will no doubt be able to detect my presence."

Morain flicked a glance at one of his advisors and Jax felt a loosening in his chest as the man bowed and moved away.

So far, so good. The King wasn't blood-red and ordering for his cock on a pike yet. Jax dared to lower his mental shields and sensed anger and disgust but it was directed at Kyrel, not himself. The King believed him.

"She kept me without food or a female companion—"

"What?" Morain growled, rising slowly from his throne. The blood was bad enough, that would starve him. But an ungelded male vampire needed more than the blood, he needed the sex. The hormones that pumped through his body would drive him mad if he didn't have the sex. They needed it.

Not just wanted, but needed. Once a vampire reached his or her prime in their thirties, sex was as important to their wellbeing as blood. Unless gelded before they hit their prime, sex became a need, as important to a vampire as feeding, as breathing. Without it, the vampire's body would turn on him, as the hormones built and built, slowly turning into a poison that destroyed the mind.

"Kyrel did what?" His hands clenched into tight fists and his eyes closed. Jax saw the denial on his face and felt his heart twist. It must be hard, learning that you had such a monster for a child. Morain had done nothing wrong, truly. Some people were just—evil. "How long?"

Jax said roughly, "Two weeks. Three days ago she came into the room, and it was the first time I had seen her since she'd had me thrown in there. She had one of the castle's magic workers preventing me from calling out to another vampire, else I would have already called for aid. She came in and cut herself, then stripped herself and painted herself with her blood."

"Did you willingly mate with her?"

"No," Jax growled, fighting down the anger. His fangs had dropped, and his eyes were burning, glowing with the rage that he couldn't suppress. But losing his temper would do him no good here. "I would have fed only but she called her guards and they took me down. While they held me, she—"

The red flush climbing up his neck told the tale and Jax turned his back. He didn't turn when he heard the small chime that signified an incoming relay. But he heard Faraman's voice and he turned his head. "My Lord King, I beg of you, I have heard of the Princess Kyrel's claims, but I have proof—"

"Proof is not necessary, but I fear, for my own good, I will have to see it," Morain said, nodding to the golden-haired man in the relay window. "What is this proof, nephew mine?"

"I've been watching how bad the Princess has become around him, how deviously she plots to get him. You know how little I trust her." Faraman paused and Jax heard the second small humming beep as a different sort of relay came in and was accepted.

"Jax is going to be mad—hell, he's going to be fucking furious, Uncle, but I rigged his clothing with a relay device and I caught the whole bloody show. Watch it if you must, or have an advisor watch it for you, but be warned, it will turn your stomach," Faraman told his uncle. "My cousin bloody raped him and she had her guards beat him. I said nothing until she voiced her accusations, because I knew what Jax's feelings would be on the issue. But with his life possibly at stake, I cannot hold my silence."

"If you had him rigged, you knew he was being held captive," Morain said slowly, his bushy gray brows lowered over his eyes.

Faraman sighed and said, "Indeed. But I wanted proof of her treachery, something that I could use against her to keep her from stalking him. Jax would not dare to speak against a human—he doubts whether you'd believe him."

Faraman's voice chilled and he said, "I have no such qualms."

Jax would have cheerfully beaten his best friend at the moment. So now his shame was for the whole fucking court to know.

Later, as he refused the offer of a bed mate from one of the courtiers, he fought off the increasing sense of restlessness and rage. Morain had sent Jax to the healers, but Morain looked like he needed the healers more.

The King looked broken.

His beloved daughter was a whore, a murderous bitch, a viper. He had to send his own guard after her, and a brawl had ensued that had left six of the men dead. Her guard had fought, and four of the fallen were hers. The remaining eleven were under arrest, those who were badly hurt were in the hospital under guard, the rest in prison. All had known where the King's most favored Warrior was held, and none had dared to tell. None had dared to help him.

Seven had cheerfully beaten him.

Jax was going insane here.

He couldn't continue to live like this, not free, not happy, little more than a fighting machine.

There had to be more to his life than this.

Sometimes, there was a yearning that filled his heart, a need, an ache. Like he wasn't supposed to be where he was. He was so focused on that, and still so drained from the beating and two weeks of starvation, that he let the footsteps behind him go unnoticed.

By the time he was struck on the head, it was too late.

He awoke just in time to realize he was restrained, once more, by the verstael restraints, and two men, lovers of the Princess', were carrying him outside. And the dual orange suns were rising, the deep fatigue rolling through his mind.

Just then, a soft, half desperate voice whispered, in his mind, *Damn it, you're supposed to be here. Come and find me!*

That voice...it stirred him, called to him. It felt like...home.

In his panic, Jax gave a desperate laugh. *Too late, darling. I'm about to become nothing more than ashes.*

Chapter Three
The Arrival

Caris knew the moment she awoke something had happened. She woke slowly, feeling something subtle, but powerful, something life-altering. She just hoped she hadn't done anything major. She had been watching a special on Egypt one time on the news screen, one of her passions. She was so fascinated by that ancient, forgotten time and had one time fallen asleep wishing that Sphinxes hadn't fallen into so much decay. Egyptologists to this day still couldn't figure out how the damaged monoliths had been one day nearly fallen to pieces and then the next, pristine and untouched.

A miracle, some called it.

A hoax, others said.

A pity.

A scandal.

It had been dubbed anything and everything in between.

Her major gift was one a teacher had taken to calling dreaming. Sometimes, things she dreamed and wished for simply came true. But they had to be true and heartfelt. And they so rarely happened. She hated it. It was useless. What did it matter if she fell asleep the day before her prom, wishing she could have a dress she had seen, and it was there the next day? Could she bring her parents back?

No.

Could she stop the world from hating them?

No.

Anything that truly, truly mattered—could she stop it? Change it? Fix it?

No.

What she wanted was for the children to stop living in terror. For them to stop dying. And no matter how many times she dreamed it, wished it, it never happened.

Sage had told her once, in his deep gravelly voice, her dreamings were things that affected her, or those around her, or small populations. She couldn't affect the whole fucking world. What was the point, then? He had smiled as he stroked her naked back, soothing her into sleep, preferably a deep, dreamless one, and whispered softly, "We don't know yet. But we will find out."

Caris swung her legs over the chair, wincing. She shouldn't have fallen asleep like that. She arched her arms up high, working the kinks out of her back. She eyed the book lying on the floor and nibbled her lower lip. No more reading before falling asleep.

But damn it…she was horny. Sage came around less and less. And she was selective. She had to be. Even among the Firewalkers. Sleeping with a man who wasn't an empath or telepath could be a painful experience—they often thought, "her breasts are too small, or too big, or is her hair really that color? Damn it, she knows how to suck, or I wish she'd suck longer". She couldn't block when she was touching someone. An empath could link with her and all they felt was the pleasure. Another telepath could think whatever the hell he chose, but if he was feeling critical, he could at least keep her from hearing him. The nicer ones at least bothered to do so.

The jerks never did.

Ungifted men were painful lessons she no longer tried.

She moved around the house first.

Nothing changed there.

Then it had to be outside. If she didn't find anything there, she'd check the news later. Somewhere, she'd find something that had changed. But the only thing she could remember thinking was wishing for a —

A vampire. Just then, a rough, deep male bellow sounded from outside. Followed by a stream of liquid language that she had never heard before. Oh, shit.

* * * * *

Jax bellowed, flinging his arms in front of his face. A blinding vortex of light and dark swirled around him and he felt as though he was being pulled into a million pieces. And that voice, the yearning female's voice, *Damn it, you're supposed to be here. Come and find me!*

He kept waiting for the burning to start.

He landed on something and smelled grass, not the stench of his own flesh burning. He felt warmth on his face, warmth, not painful burning. The dual suns of Oslina hurt. He had felt them before. His fear and the vampire's instinct for survival kicked in, chasing away the fatigue.

Awake and aware, he could possibly find a place to hide if they hadn't taken him into the desert. So now, he'd be awake for his own burning as the fear in his body chased away the chemicals that rose with the sun, the chemicals that drugged him into a catatonic sleep.

I'd rather sleep through it, thank you very much...

It would take time for the suns to char his flesh from his body, but Kyrel's men would have taken him far into the deserts and the suns would have plenty of time.

But when he felt only a slight stinging, and no pain, he opened first one eye, then the other.

One sun. Yellow, not orange. Grass, not sand.

Mountains in the distance, covered on the caps with snow, soft grass under his body, and a large, sprawling wooden-framed structure. There was a woman there, and she was staring at him with big, wide golden eyes, the color of the Altamyrian moon, her pink lips parted.

While he watched, she lifted one fisted hand and pressed it to her lips, still staring at him with those amazing eyes. Jax rolled onto his back, staring up into the sun, for the first time in his life, with amazement. It did not burn his flesh, and he felt no fear of it. And the sleep that should have closed in on him as his fear faded didn't occur.

Astounding.

But more astounding was when the woman who should have been running and screaming, came and knelt by his side, her brow puckered. Her mouth opened and she spoke, but he shook his head. He knew the sentiment, he could feel it coming from her. She wanted to know if he was all right. But until she touched him, or he her, he wouldn't know her tongue.

His body tightened. Her tongue. Before, it had just meant the language of the land. But suddenly it meant more.

He received another shock, in a day that was apparently meant to be full of them, when her mind brushed his. She was a psy, like him. *I'm not going to hurt you*, she was telling him more, in pictures and thoughts instead of words. She showed him how she wanted to undo the restraints but didn't know how.

He responded in kind, showing her the locking mechanism, but he didn't expect her to grasp the concept.

More the fool he, he realized when he was rolling to his feet moments later. He wanted to thank her.

But first, he turned and stared hard, at the pale yellow orb, harsh and shining, high overhead. So many years of artificial light, of moonlight, starlight, firelight. So many years of falling prey to the drug of sleep as the sun rose.

The sunlight...never had he been in the sunlight without cowering, flinging his arms over his face, wondering if that would be his last moment. He had been tortured with it, thrown into it in battle by his captors and taunted with it by his enemies, but never had he been able to simply stand and absorb it without fear.

It made his sensitive eyes water and hurt. He could feel his flesh, after fifty years of night, going pink, but he continued to bask in the warmth. The moon, well, it was lovely, but he had never seen anything as glorious as this sun.

Slowly, he turned and studied the woman in front of him who was staring at him with her dark, golden eyes. Her eyes and hair were nearly the same color, golden-brown, warm looking. She had tiny freckles, like gold dust across her nose, a pink, plump mouth, a heart-shaped face. A tall, slender body that curved exactly where it should, and long, sleekly muscled thighs showing beneath the hem of her white shirt, the only garment that she wore.

Her mouth moved and he shook his head. Then he held out his hand, focusing his thoughts. *Touch my hand?*

He projected the thought at her, hoping she would understand. She was human, but there was something different, he could scent it on her skin, in her blood. The humans he knew had no PSY skills, but many had magic. This wasn't exactly magic he was tasting in the air, it was something unique.

She smiled slowly, and lifted her hand. He wondered if she could read him and suspected, by the glint in her eyes, that she could. He placed his palm to hers, folding his fingers around it.

Her back arched, his arched, they fell against each other and sagged to their knees on the ground, as Jax took her language inside him. Bits and pieces of her flowing into him before he could stop it, and no doubt, bits and pieces of his life flooding into her brain.

* * * * *

He may not be a vampire, but he was something. His gaze stared into hers, glowing and hot, filling her entire field of vision until those magnificent sapphire eyes were all she could see. She felt his hand — hot, hard, rough — slide over hers, over her wrist, up her arm, over her shoulder. It lingered on her neck, and he shuddered.

She felt some massive need roll over him but he moved on until he cupped her cheek in one hand, then the other, so that he held her face in both, while he stared down at her as though fascinated.

She understood that. Her mind was full to bursting with what she had gleaned from his mind as he touched her, information that she couldn't make sense of.

His head was lowering.

He was going to kiss her.

Oh, damn.

Her muscles turned to water when his lips, warm and soft, pressed against hers, chastely at first, then more firmly, as he used his hands to arch her head and neck. She opened her mouth and felt heat pool in her belly, spill through her veins as his tongue thrust past her lips and teeth to taste her. One hand slid through her thick hair, holding her tight while the other slid down her body and brought her flush against him.

His body was hard and solid and real. She really wasn't dreaming this. Or dreaming it. It was real. He was real. He wedged one thigh between hers, wrapping one thick forearm around her waist while a deep, rough growl rippled out of his chest.

The sound made her wet. She started to rock against him, riding his thigh hungrily. The thin barrier of her panties against the slick material of his black pants made it easy. She shuddered when both hands suddenly clamped on her hips and started to drag her back and forth, angling her body so that her clit was given the royal treatment with each stroke against his solid, muscled thigh.

His mouth ate at hers, she felt a sharp, fleeting pain, and tasted blood.

Then, suddenly, she was standing there, on shaking legs, her head spinning from being moved so fast and he was ten feet away, panting and staring at her with eyes that glowed. She felt blood rush to her head, felt the slow throb of need as it pulsed through her loins and a hungry whimpering died in her throat.

"I beg your pardon," he said slowly. The words were slow, obviously foreign. His accent was beyond bizarre, like nothing she had ever heard, but his words were unmistakably English.

* * * * *

Mate.

Every instinct in his body cried it, but Jax just stared at the slim, small woman who stared back at him, her eyes cloudy and hazed with hunger, her soft mouth kiss-swollen. He had damn near done the unforgivable and fed without permission.

It was the one crime he knew Morain's ancestors had been right to ban. But he had never wanted to sink his fangs into a tender, warm neck so badly.

It mattered little that he was no longer in his world.

Or even in his own galaxy.

He suspected some odd magic was at work. Even on other worlds, the sun was death to his kind. It produced a rise in the chemical that regulated his body functions, the one that slowed metabolism, and forced his body into a near coma state, even when he was hidden away from its direct rays. The law of natural selection at its finest — it forced him to sleep, leaving him vulnerable.

And the rays were deadly, able to slowly burn his body to ash, yet he stood here, in the glare of the sun and felt...fine.

He was in some other time or dimension. How or why, he didn't know. But nothing gave him the right to take without permission. Especially considering he suspected this woman was how he had come to be here. And if that was so, then he owed her his life.

Mate, the animal inside him insisted. Feed. Mark. Breed. Jax shoved it aside and down, taking a deep breath, scenting the clean grass, smelling the sunshine, and her. "I beg your pardon," he said slowly, forcing the unfamiliar words past his fangs and his tight throat. All he wanted to do was go to her, wrap her long golden hair around his hand, expose her neck and feed as he drove his cock inside her slim body.

She reached up, touched her lip, the cut that sullenly oozed blood and stared at him. "Damn," she whispered. Then she squinted up at the sun, before looking back at him. His fangs were unmistakable and he could see the knowledge, the recognition in her eyes. So his kind weren't unheard of here, wherever here was. He caught flashes from her mind, men in capes, castles in dark mountains, her own yearnings, and oddly, pictures of them, him together with her.

"The sun...?"

"Your sun apparently cannot hurt me," he said, closing his hands into loose fists. "I am not...from here. I know not how I came to this...Earth?" he asked, searching the knowledge of her language. "Where I am from, the twin suns are deadly, and I have always feared them. I thought, when I opened my eyes, death was there."

She smiled, and it was lovely. It bloomed and made her face sparkle and glow. "That's good news, then, I'd think."

He gave a half-smile in return, still uncertain of her reaction to his small sip of her blood. Glancing at the golden sun, he said, "Good news? Yes. Yes. Good. Always, have I wanted to see the sun. It is a wonderful sight." He forced his eyes back to her face, and swallowed. He had suffered too many humiliations of late, and his pride was bruised. "I meant no harm, nor disrespect, when I kissed you."

Her smile grew, and a dimple flirted around her mouth. There was also a tiny little mole right beside her right eye. Jax felt his heart squeeze tight. She was adorable, truly. "I took none. I'm kinda sorry you stopped," she drawled, moving a step or two in his direction.

"I...ah, my kind—where we are from—my kind are governed strictly. We are treated as little more than slaves and we are feared. We cannot feed or touch without permission," he said, speaking more and more rapidly as she moved closer. She smelled warm and sweet.

She stopped and cocked her head, and he felt the light touch of her as she studied him. Reaching out with her own gift she took more of him into her, feeling the frustration that ate at him. He was forced to be other than what he was, to act like a weaker being, to let others control him because they feared his kind, seeing bits and pieces of his life, she read him.

Then a sad little smile curved her mouth. "Then we have a lot in common, I think." She brushed her hair back and said, "My name is Caris Montgomery. And I'd really like to know how you can speak English. A few minutes ago, I would have sworn you didn't know how."

"Caris. That's...lovely. I am Jax Regale." He dared to reach out and touch her forehead and she didn't seem to mind. The bands around his gut loosened and he wondered at it. Was he truly free here? "I'm psy. I believe you call it psychic here and you have a similar gift yourself. I can take any person's language with a touch, knowing enough to converse in the tongue. I do not know all that you know, but I know enough," he told her.

"A neat trick," she mused. "None of my friends can do that. It would be handy." She caught his hand before he could pull away and brought it back to her face.

Jax groaned as she stepped up to him and pressed her mouth to his, this time driving her tongue into his mouth, and sliding her arms around his waist, as she whispered into his mind, *I have been waiting for you for years.*

Chapter Four

Caris felt his hands go under her bottom and he boosted her up, carrying her to the house, unerringly. Once there, she reached behind her without taking her mouth from his and opened the door. He stumbled inside, kicking the door closed and pulling his mouth from hers.

She stared at his profile while he looked around, searching. The sharp tips of his fangs had descended to just past his lower lip and he kept his mouth open and his lips parted as he sucked air in rapidly. His skin was golden, warm-looking, his eyes blue. Under the glistening black material of his short, rather military looking jacket, his shoulders were wide, his torso and waist slim but muscled. She had her legs locked firmly around his waist, so she knew pretty well how it felt. Silken skeins of hair flowed past his shoulders halfway down his back, deep chestnut brown, threaded through with streaks of pure, dark red. His skin gleamed a mellow gold and was like silk over steel under her hands.

"Where?" he groaned in frustration, turning his gaze back to her. "And what am I allowed?"

Allowed? She forced herself to keep her shields up, so he wouldn't feel the streak of pity. This was a dominant creature, and he had been forced into near slavery because he was feared for his strength. He had been treated even worse than the Firewalkers had, she mused. At least they didn't have to worry about begging permission to eat and drink...they may have to hide in plain sight for that right, but they could do it. Cupping his face, she kissed him, sucking his tongue into her mouth. She delicately touched her tongue to his fangs and shuddered.

He was real…

He tore his mouth from her and went to her ear, biting down gently and growling, "Yes, I am real and if you do not intend to allow this, then I have to stop now before I lose myself."

"I've been waiting for you my whole life," she whispered. "Why wouldn't I allow it? But I don't like that word—it doesn't suit you. If I didn't want this, would I be here?" She wiggled her butt to emphasize and he groaned. "If it's permission you feel you need, then it's granted, as long as whatever you have planned doesn't involve pain. Well, lots of pain." She gave him a cheeky smile and said, "A little pain is okay."

Jax stared at her, vaguely dumbfounded.

With a sigh, she wriggled out of his tight grasp and pulled her shirt over her head. All she wore under it was a green lacy thong and a golden Celtic knot. It was a marker of sorts, among the Firewalkers. "I think we need to talk, but right now, I want to finish what we started outside. Including feeding," she said, reaching up slowly, waiting to see how he reacted, as she touched her finger to one of his fangs. "You have no idea how long I've been dreaming you…"

The same deep rumbling growl escaped him and he lunged, taking her to the floor, rolling so that she landed on him when they fell. Then she was rolled and pinned under his weight as he moved onto her lightning quick. His mouth was everywhere, and his big, wide hands moved over her like a branding iron, plucking her nipples, gripping her hips, stroking her clit before two fingers delved deeply inside her aching cleft.

His mouth followed and it was like her dream. She screamed as he finger-fucked her to climax just as he bit down at the crease between groin and thigh, his big body shaking as her blood flowed into him. He continued to work his fingers inside her tight, slippery sheath as he sucked and fed ravenously, and she whimpered as another climax built.

Each draw of his mouth on her flesh throbbed in her clit, teasing, tantalizing, pushing her closer and closer to the edge as he pumped his fingers in and out of her tight, narrow, passage.

A second orgasm started to hover over her, a sweet, seductive promise that drew her body tighter and tighter as she lifted her hips to his hand.

Just as she was reaching it, he pulled his mouth from her thigh, placed a thumb over the tiny puncture wound and caught her clit in his mouth, feasting hungrily. Her hands slid down and buried in his hair, the coppery brown strands twining over her fingers as she rocked up against him, shuddering and pleading. He stabbed at her with his tongue and shifted so he could stare up the length of her body at her.

Divine. You taste like fine wine, sweet sex, like heaven. Come, now, and let me taste that, he purred into her mind. He had taken his fingers from her body to cover and seal the wound from his feeding, but shifted now, replaced them with his other hand, working two fingers deep inside. *You like this, yes? What is the word in your tongue...fucking, yes, I could happily do this all day, feeding on your sweet cream, and fucking your tiny little channel with my fingers.*

With a scream, she came, sobbing as she rocked up against his mouth, against his hand. "Jax," she whispered, pulling at him.

He laughed against her flesh and pulled away. "Maybe no," he said, the words falling from his mouth awkwardly from the unfamiliar tongue and his lust. "Sweet, so sweet you are." He shed his clothes while kneeling between her thighs, staring at her, at the plump folds of her sex, at the already healing bite mark, as he struggled out of the formfitting black jacket. His long fingers found some hidden tab on the trousers, opened it, and Caris gasped as his cock sprang free, thick and long with a ruddy tip, nestled in a thatch of dark coppery hair.

His body was lean, corded with muscle, hard and perfect. Caris watched him hungrily as he shoved his pants down just past his slim hips and covered her, taking her mouth hungrily. His fangs had pulled back a bit and he slanted his mouth so that they did little more than press against her as he kissed her, sucking her tongue into his mouth, biting down greedily as he probed at her wet cleft. *I want to feel all of you*, he whispered hungrily into her mind. *You have strong mental blocks and I know not why.*

Caris tunneled her fingers through his hair, hesitantly dropping the shields as he caught one thigh in his hand, held her behind the knee and brought it up over his hip. Her breath caught on a sob as he pierced her and drove in, filling her tight sheath, stretching her wet tissues, until she thought she would burst.

Jax murmured softly against her mouth, foreign exotic words, while one hand stroked her hair. Rolling his weight to one side, he reached down and found her clit, rolling it gently, then more quickly as he kissed his way down her chin to the curve of her neck and shoulder. There he nipped her, light and quick, not even breaking the surface, and when her eyes opened wide, and her back arched with shock at the sudden sharp pain, he pulled out and drove his thick cock completely in.

Caris whimpered and sobbed, writhing under him. He caught her thrashing head in his hands and kissed her roughly, hungrily, greedily, thrusting his tongue deep inside her mouth. Forcing her mouth as wide open as he could, taking as much of her taste as he could gather, he held still, waiting for her snug, tight sheath to accommodate him. She was silky, wet, creamy. Her hands curled into his biceps, clenching convulsively, while she whimpered deep in her throat. The solid, sturdy shields she had around her soul, her mind were dissolving and Jax could feel his soul sinking into hers as his cock nestled into her sweet little pussy.

The head of his cock pulsed inside her, vibrated against her G-spot and Caris sobbed against his mouth, twining her legs around his waist and rubbing against him hungrily. He pulled away, half laughing, half groaning as he started to ride her, one big hand cupping her hip, her ass, the other flat beside her head, holding his big, heavy body off of her as they stared into each other's eyes.

"Jax—oh, please, there, oh!" she wailed when he twisted his hips a certain way, rubbing right against her clit with the downstroke.

"Do not close your eyes, Caris," he whispered gruffly. "I want to see you." Her lids lifted slowly, sleepily and she stared back up him, a whimper falling from her lips as he pulled out and worked back in, forced to fight the gradual resistance of her wet, tight sheath as she clenched around him in climax. "Such a sweet thing you are..."

"More," she pleaded, reaching up and wrapping her arms around his neck. "Please, more. I've been waiting for you for so long."

Jax groaned and crushed his mouth to hers, taking her slim hips in his big hands, pounding into her, forcing himself to some restraint, but shuddering at the tight, sweet grip of her pussy on his cock, flicking his thumb over her swollen clit as he drove back inside.

That silky wet pussy closed over him and he growled hungrily, pulling out and sinking back again, and again, shuddering each time she enveloped him, hot, hungry, like a greedy fist.

Her legs clamped strongly around his waist, and she started to come, a slow, gradual storm that built and built, until her shuddering rhythmic milking had him bellowing and driving into her like a wild thing. It wasn't until it was too late that he realized he was coming inside her, filling her tight receptive body with his sperm. When he tried to pull out, she locked her arms around him, recognizing the intention if not the reason, and kissed him hungrily as she rubbed her pelvis against his, so that he felt the hard little swell of her clit. He swore and gave up, flooding her with his seed and reveling in the freedom to do so.

Long moments passed before his mind was clear enough to think. Lying with his head on her breasts, Jax's mind chased itself in wearying circles, the who, the what, and the how started to build.

Not right now, he muttered to himself. *Just for a while, let me take this in.*

* * * * *

Caris felt the tight swell of power in the air only moments before Sage was there. She sat up slowly, drawing the sheet up, as she kept a hand on Jax's chest. Sage and she were off and on lovers, more off than on lately, but he was her friend, and he cared about her. He might not react well to seeing another man in her bed, not out of jealousy, but more out of the need to protect.

Sage tended to take protecting her rather seriously.

The teleporter exploded into the room with a burst of light, going from wherever he had been causing trouble to causing trouble here. *Lucky me*, Caris thought.

Jax's body tensed as he sensed the chaos in her mind, as he sensed the swelling of power in the room, and she pressed her fingers into his arm and whispered, "It's all right. He's a friend."

And then Sage was there, his hair caught in a stubby black tail, his fox-like, elegant face shadowed by a day's growth of beard. He had large widely-spaced hazel eyes that flicked from Caris to Jax and back to Caris. High cheekbones, a pointed chin, every feature on his face sharp and defined, the skin gleaming a mellow gold. His body was long and lean, deadly, capable of moving with a nearly blinding speed.

Right now, his eyes were narrowed as he settled back against the door and hooked his thumbs in the loops of his worn jeans.

Jax's heart was racing and she could feel his shock. Wherever he was from, teleporters weren't something he was familiar with, she decided. It wasn't a common thing here, but she suspected he was covering a very serious shock.

"Look at what we have here," Sage murmured, shaking his head. He cocked a brow at Caris and said, "You going for the prettier ones now?"

She smiled sunnily and said, "Sorry, babe. I can't handle you not shaving. You're going to peel the skin from me one of these days."

"Ouch," he said mildly, rubbing a thumb over his chin. "Sorry to interrupt. We have a problem. You're needed. Tell lover-boy buh-bye for now, Sugar. We got to roll."

Jax's eyes narrowed and he propped himself up on his elbow as he glared at Sage. His mouth opened but Caris laid two fingers against his lips and shook her head, smiling a little. "I'm not leaving him if I'm going out for a job, Sage. He comes," she said, looking back at her friend.

Sage's eyes narrowed and he stared at Jax. "He's not one of us, Sugar. You want to sleep with him, fine. He may well be a decent guy and if he's not, that's your concern and none of mine. But he's not one of us, so no can do. He's not coming."

"He's closer than you think, Sage. And yes, he is."

She felt the waves of confusion from this conversation that rolled from Jax and she found his hand in the sheets and held it while she focused her thoughts and projected them for Jax alone.

Do you remember that neat little trick I admired so much?

I do, yes. Slow amusement, like a reluctant chuckle, followed his reply.

Can you use it for more than languages?

I have never tried, for certain. But I would believe so.

Good. There is something I need to fill you in on, but not now. It will be quicker that way. She looked back at Sage who was glaring irritably at her. He knew what the signs of silent conversations were and he was listening but hearing nothing. Caris was a powerful telepath, but only another receiver could hear her thoughts when she was shielding tightly. Which meant only one thing.

"You aren't one of us," Sage said, shaking his head. "I know what a Firewalker feels like in my head. And you're not it. But you don't feel…human either. And you can hear her. The ungifted can only hear us when we go on broadcast."

Caris slid closer to Jax, cuddling into the curve of his body. "He's not. But he's no threat to me, or to our kind, Sage. I brought him here," she whispered, still half in awe of that. "I brought him here. If he was a threat to us, I couldn't have done that."

"Brought him?" Sage repeated. Jax's body stiffened.

She felt the light, intimate touch of his mind on hers as he breathed his thoughts into her. *I knew it, I felt it.* His arms folded tightly around her and she felt the shudder that racked his body.

Sage sighed, pressing the heels of his hands to his eyes. "The dreaming?" he asked quietly, walking to the chair by the bed and throwing his long, rangy body into it. His eyes darkened thoughtfully, broodingly. The dreaming wasn't dangerous, or it hadn't been yet, but this was new. Caris had wished herself new clothes as a child, had fixed ancient crumbling statues in her dreaming, and had from time to time used the dreaming to bring a captured or injured comrade out of harm's way.

But she had never used it to bring somebody who wasn't of this world into it before.

"Yes," Caris said. She had to focus. A battering ram of emotion was flowing off of Jax to her and it tightened her throat, made it hard to think. All she wanted to do was turn around and climb onto him, hold on tight while he thrust his cock up into her. Fuck Sage. He could watch or he could go.

But he had said she was needed.

"What's gone wrong?" she forced herself to ask.

"The boy I took this morning. Something's been done to him. He's locked in and we don't know why. There's something not right. Ari can't come and Kelly has somebody who's been hurt that she can't leave," Sage said, staring up at the ceiling, his fist closed and pounding on the arm of the chair. "Morgan sent me to get you. We need you, Caris."

She sighed and pulled away from Jax. "I didn't say I wouldn't come, Sage. I just said I wasn't coming without Jax."

"Jax," Sage repeated, rolling his eyes. He shoved up out of the chair and stalked out of the room, his long black duster whirling around his ankles. "Jax," he mumbled under his breath, shaking his head. "Are you going to get dressed or what, Sugar?"

"Sugar?" Jax repeated.

"Are you two having fun parroting the other?" Caris asked as she reluctantly climbed out of bed. She winced, moving gingerly. Jax had been greedy and hungry and had taken her time and again throughout the night.

"Parroting?"

"Acting like a parrot," she clarified absently as she gathered clothing. Raising her voice she shouted into the living room, "Sage! I'm taking a bath. Morgan can wait long enough for that, right?"

"A bath?" She heard his mumbling reply but not a negative and moved into the bathroom off her bedroom, glancing at the vampire still sprawled on her bed.

"So now I am a bird?" Jax asked, his brows drawn together.

"Acting like a parrot, repeating everything back to you. 'Jax, Sugar, bath'," she mumbled, deepening her voice, mocking Sage and Jax. She bent over the tub and started the water and felt two big warm hands smoothing over her ass. With a whimper, she pushed back against him, unable to resist. "Shouldn't you know what that means anyway?"

Jax laughed. "A new language, confusing, this one. Would you like to try adding a fiftieth language to your mind, and not get confused?" he teased as he nudged his cock against her backside.

The pounding rush of water flowing into the sunken tub covered the sound of her gasp as he slid two fingers inside her tightly swollen cleft, sore, sensitive from being ridden all night. "Jax, I've got to hurry—"

"Then I shall," he murmured, wedging his thigh between hers to widen her stance and driving deep, tunneling through her pussy all the way to her core in one stroke.

Jax stared at the slim line of her pale back, at the curve of her ass, watching at he worked his cock back inside her slippery, tight channel. She held him so snuggly, her heat so creamy, so soft. His cock gleamed wet with her cream, and his balls ached. Pulling out, he shuddered as he pushed back inside the tight, wet core, burying himself to the balls inside, listening to the hungry mewling sound coming from her throat. Over the rushing water, the sounds of their loving would not carry to the man Sage, and Jax wished he had turned off the water.

They had been lovers.

They would not be again.

This woman was his. He gripped her hips and slammed into her as his fangs dropped. He should not be hungry again, not for blood, not now. But the scent of her arousal, the sound of her pounding heart called to him as he stroked the pearl just above her slit and felt her quiver. "You stretch so tightly around me, Caris," he murmured in praise, stroking the soft lips of her sex, gliding his fingers over her clit. He thrust deep, pushed her hips a little lower. "Hot and sweet, your pussy..."

"Ohhhh," she whimpered, bracing her hands on the rim of the deep tub, her voice barely audible over the sound of the water. Hmmm....he did like the sound of her moaning. He should most definitely have turned the water off.

Pulling out, he drove back in, setting a quick, hungry pace, reaching around to tug and stroke her clit. Her long tawny hair spilled around her golden body, and her slender back arched as he shifted his angle to rub against the notch deep inside that would make her sob with pleasure.

When he had her rocking and riding his fingers, he jerked her torso up, holding her against him and fucking her with short deep digs of his hips, taking one of her hands and urging her fingers to her cleft, to the swollen nub of her clit as he burrowed back inside. He wound her hair around his hand and bared her neck, licking it hungrily.

Her head fell back and she sobbed, shoving her ass against his hips as hard as she could, moaning and whimpering roughly as his fangs raked her neck. The long, perfect line of her body lay naked to his eyes, the roundness of her breasts, her concave little belly, her fingers circling around her clit, gleaming wet with her cream.

"May I?" he groaned against her ear.

She half laughed, half swore. "I told you, you don't have to ask," she rasped, rolling her head to the side.

The sweet burning pleasure of his fangs breaking her skin was the last sensation she needed as she stroked her fingers rapidly over her clit and she bit her lip to muffle the scream as she climaxed around him, squeezing the thick, hard cock buried deep inside her. His come, hot and molten, jetted off inside her and she shuddered and cried, reaching behind her and winding one arm around his neck as he fed, holding him tightly against her.

He still fed at her neck as he lifted her up and took her into the bath, his stiff cock still nestled snug inside her pussy. She whimpered and shifted against him as he settled them down in the bath, water spilling over onto the floor as he turned it off before reluctantly drawing away from her neck. He pressed his lips to the wound this time, sealing it slowly with his kiss, licking away the lingering drops.

Drowsily, she asked, "Don't take this wrong, but do you ever lose this?" She squeezed his cock gingerly with her inner muscles. He puzzled out her question by touching her mind with his while he combed his hands through her hair and once he had her meaning his jaw clenched. "I have hurt you."

"No. I'm just a little sore," she said, snuggling herself more firmly against him as he tried to move away.

She felt the shame, saw it in his eyes. "I...I have never been able to claim a woman for my own for anything more than a few hours, or a night. It is not a right my kind are easily given. But that does not give me the right to abuse—"

"There's been no abuse," she cut him off by pressing her mouth to his. "Something tells me your anatomy is just a little more powerful than mine. I'm not hurt. I've just never been one to participate in all night fuckfests."

His mouth curved in a slow smile, and she felt her heart twist. Damn it, what were they thinking, trying to hold someone like him captive? Hugging him briefly she moved away and slipped beneath the water to wet her hair. She washed hurriedly, all too aware that Sage would grow impatient and barge in, either through the door, or using his less than traditional means.

Jax sat, just watching her, and once she had climbed out, he washed, quickly, economically. "I love baths," she told him as she smoothed a towel over her body. "I had to pay to have this put in, and to have the water line laid down. Some people have never taken a bath like this, not on this planet. They use more mundane means of bathing these days."

She ran the towel quickly over her hair, slathered some gel through it so it would dry well—the thick golden hair was straight, but the texture was actually so fine, she either had use the gel or take the time to dry it out, or it tended to dry in stringy clumps.

Caris tossed the towel over the heated bar before grabbing her lotion. Out of the corner of her eye, she watched him rise from the bath, the water rolling from his golden body, down his flat belly, his cock, off of thick heavily muscled thighs. Swallowing, Caris dragged her eyes away and smoothed the vanilla lotion over her arms and legs.

He was drying himself using her towel, and watching her with hot, hungry eyes, his coppery brown hair nearly black as it hung down, plastered to his shoulders in wet streaming ribbons. The hard carved perfection of his chest and belly drew her eye as water streamed down his body.

Lifting the towel to his head to sop up the water from his hair, he paused and drew in the scent of it, closing his eyes. "You smell sweet, like spring, like rain," he murmured, lifting his head to stare at her with eyes that looked glassy, almost drugged.

Caris shuddered. *Damn it, he's distracting.* Then he lowered his lashes and shook his head, breaking the spell. She escaped from the bathroom before she threw herself at him. Even though the muscles in her thighs ached, even though her vagina felt raw and battered now, looking at him made her hungry, made her yearn all over again.

He left the bathroom as she was shimmying into a slim fitting pair of black jeans. She topped it with a white tank and white sleeveless top before sliding her feet into air-soled sandals. You never knew when your job was going to take you on serious walk detail so she generally tried to dress comfortably. She pulled a jacket out after recalling the duster Sage had worn and hoped they were not going someplace cold.

Summer had just come to Montana and she wasn't looking forward to leaving the beauty of it for any reason, much less for a cold place. Jax stood watching her with his head cocked, a half smile on his face, the towel hooked around his hips. "My clothing is in the other—" she watched his eyes close, the look she recognized now that he was searching his mind for the proper word. How many languages did he know? "The living room? Why a living room? Is there one not living?"

A laugh bubbled out of her throat and she shook her head. "No. That's just what we call it. It's kind of our focal point, our social area," she responded, flipping her damp hair off her shoulders. "I'll bring it in here."

She was brushing past him when he laid one hand on her shoulder. "I will come out there with you," he said. His eyes were dark, troubled pools of blue, studying her face. "This...this Sage is a lover of yours?"

"Ah, hmmm. On occasion, yes."

His fingers curled into her shoulder and his eyes narrowed, his face tightened and Caris watched as it transformed into that of a predator. His fangs dropped down protruding past his upper lip and flashing at her as he backed her against the wall. "Will these occasions stop?" he asked, his voice dropping to a growl.

He was struggling to control a beast that was raging inside him, Caris thought. How had a planet of humans managed to enslave creatures like him? He was so completely dominant. She closed the scant inches between them and wrapped her arms around his neck, lowering her shields, allowing her mind to mesh with his. What she wanted to say was too complex.

She was fond of Sage. He was a good lover and he had helped keep the loneliness at bay. Loneliness for a dreamer wasn't a good thing.

But she had been waiting for Jax.

Waiting for him to come and find her, claim her, love her. She had been waiting for him, had suffered alone through a million fantasies, and she focused on them, funneling them through the meshing of their minds and pouring them into his. He wasn't enslaved here, he didn't have to ask permission to do a damn thing, and she was waiting for him to claim and take and mark her.

He shuddered as he plundered her mouth with his, one fang nicking her lip as he rocked his cock against her covered cleft. *This was not a wise time to share such with me. I should have waited on this,* he rasped into her mind. With a savage groan he tore his mouth from hers and licked away the blood before putting distance between them.

"You make me lose all control, Caris," he said, shaking his head. It was reeling from the things she had pushed into his mind. She wanted no subjugation, wanted no submissiveness or subservience. But aggression and dominance, the traits he had been forced to suppress in all but battle for his fifty years of life.

Her dreams, her fantasies, they had all seemed to focus around him, before she had ever met him, before she had pulled him here. Claiming. She wanted him to claim her. *I will,* he purred into her mind, afraid to move close and touch her again just yet. *But now is not the time.*

She was still trembling minutely when he followed her from the room into the larger living room—such an odd phrase. But Caris assured him there was no dying room. Sage was stalking around the room in tight, controlled circles. This man, he had much, much anger inside him. When he stopped and turned to look at Caris, Jax had to force himself to breathe slowly, to think past the rage he felt as he imagined this other man bedding Caris— bedding his woman—to the gentleness he saw in the human's gaze, the urge to protect and keep safe.

"Nice clothes," Sage drawled, glancing at Jax. Jax watched blandly as he walked to where his flight suit lay on the floor. He dropped the towel and picked up his trousers, donning the smooth veltec as he concentrated on retracting his fangs. He had fed twice, and he had bedded Caris a number of times, so he shouldn't be easily enraged. But his rage didn't want to subside. He slid his hand over the seam and it closed over his groin before he took his jacket and donned it. His fangs slowly started to pull up into their sheaths behind his canines. By the time he had closed the seam of the flight jacket, the fangs had retracted and he could meet Sage's eyes levelly before returning his gaze to the floor to find his boots.

"Interesting clothing. Into leather?" Sage murmured to Caris.

Jax acted as though he hadn't heard. But he got the picture from the other man's mind. Apparently the other man didn't realize just how strong Jax's psy skills were. He saw Sage teasing Caris with a mental picture, her bound to a bed, Jax in his black flight suit, her wearing a tiny black garment resembling the veltec, that pushed her lush breasts up and out. Then another picture, Jax smacking her lily-white ass. His first thought was rage, and his fangs dropped again.

But then his cock hardened and Jax shuddered, wheeled on his bare heel, and stalked out the door into the cool morning air.

"Fuck, Sage, take out an ad on the news screen next time," Caris hissed, blushing. The images Sage had sent her had her cheeks flaming, but it was with both embarrassment and arousal.

Sage's eyes narrowed, then widened, and he grinned. "Oops."

"Can't you do anything on a level other than broadcast?" she snapped, brushing past him.

"Look, let lover-boy calm down. I'll come back after I take you to Morgan."

"Not a good idea, babe," she drawled. She turned to look at him. "He's not human. I'm not going into detail about what he is. That's his choice, his call. But he's not human. And he possesses...gifts that could make some of ours look like card tricks. He just caught every last thing you thought, Sage. Without even trying. And I suspect if he wanted, he could rip you into so many pieces, they would still be trying to piece you together when the Fire's Creator comes back to claim us."

Sage stiffened but she cut him off. "Don't. Sage, I know you. And I know more about him than you do. Trust me on this. And for God's sake, watch your manners."

"Don't have any," he returned, crossing his arms over his chest and glaring at her slim back as she walked out the door.

She was making him take Jax first. She knew Sage well enough to know he could get temperamental. If he took her first, she wouldn't put it past the teleporter to suddenly decide to claim weariness. It would be bullshit. Teleportation was like breathing to Sage, but she wouldn't put it past him.

She smoothed her hands down the shiny black of the jacket. "We're going to have to find you some clothes that call a little less attention," she mused. Then she slid him a saucy look and whispered, "But I want to keep these."

He smiled down at her, stroking one hand over her still damp golden hair.

"It's going to feel weird, like you're being pulled into a million pieces, and like you're flying through water at the same time," she told him. "It's loud and it's fast. It feels like it takes forever, but it won't. Focus on something that matters, keep it in your mind until you're there and it's over."

Jax leaned down, curling his larger frame around hers to kiss her softly. "I will focus then, on you, Caris," he murmured.

Sage watched and listened with dark, unreadable eyes, shaking his head as the vampire slowly pulled away from Caris. "I'll be back in a few, Sugar," he drawled as he moved closer to Jax. The vampire eyed him narrowly, menacingly as Sage moved into his space.

Correctly reading the warning look on Jax's face, Sage laughed. "Sorry, man, that's the way it works. Gotta get close. Don't wanna lose you on the way. Caris would never forgive me," he mocked Jax's accent sarcastically as he looped his arms under and around Jax's, so that they stood nearly eye to eye. "Damn, you are a pretty thing, ain't ya? Good thing I don't like guys. Of course, we got teleporters around who do — "

Caris covered her face with her hands to stifle her frustrated groan as they exploded and were gone.

Jax ignored Sage, focusing instead on Caris' words. Yes. It did feel like he was being pulled into a million pieces, but it had felt like that when she had brought him here. And it wasn't that much different from the jump to light-speed, except then he was secured in a ship.

Right now, he was locked against another man, something he wasn't altogether fond of, and his stomach was roiling, his head was roaring.

Focus.

He pulled Caris' face into his mind and focused on her, on her scent, her taste, her soul, the feel of her skin, her body, the snug fit of her cleft around his cock. And the feel of home that he had recognized the moment he had looked into her eyes as she stood staring at him while he waited for the sun to burn him to ashes. The sickness, the dizziness, the sensation of something trying to pull his body apart, swirled to a halt around him, and the tight grasp of Sage's arms fell away—he had to give the mortal credit. He didn't like Jax, it was quite clear. But he took his responsibility for his safety very seriously. Jax had a feeling that to falter and let loose while "teleporting" as Caris called it, would be a very, very bad thing.

He stepped away, glad to feel firm ground under his feet and looked around, seeing four more human faces staring at him with varying degrees of surprise and distrust. Sage was staring at him expectantly, but Jax couldn't figure out why until he picked up a number of pictures flashing through the dark-haired man's mind. After teleporting with Sage, people usually collapsed to the ground, nauseated and weak, sweating, sometimes vomiting. This occurred after the first, and often the second experience.

"Sorry to disappoint you," Jax murmured, shifting his shoulders a little, straightening his flight suit and skimming the faces around him with a quick eye.

Sage gave him a disgusted look before turning to the others. "This is a friend of Caris'. She was rather adamant he come with her, and before I bring her," Sage said, jerking his head in Jax's direction, "Her exact words were 'I'm not going into detail about what he is. That's his choice, his call. You want details, ask him. Not me.' Be right back."

Jax's eyes watered as a tremendous silent explosion seemed to shake the room, leaving an empty spot where

Sage had stood. He turned his head, glancing over his shoulder at the four faces that stared at him with varying degrees of surprise, ranging from mild amusement and curiosity, to downright hostility. A tall, lean man with hair the color of snow moved out of the group. If he had judged just by the hair, and maybe the weariness of his eyes, Jax would have guessed the man was easily his own age, but fifty in human years was nothing to a vampire. But the man's face was unlined, and he moved easily, confidently.

"I am Morgan," he said coolly, studying Jax with eyes the color of pale blue crystal. "I don't particularly care if Caris wanted you here or not. This is my show, and these are my agents. Who in the fuck are you?"

"Jax, my name is Jax," he replied. He kept his shields down and open, taking his cue from the more open minds around. Morgan's was not one of them. He wasn't a true psy, but there was something about him.

The swell of power filled the room, and Jax felt it, sensed it before the others. Sage and Caris were about to return, yet the others didn't feel them coming. If they had, he believed they would have left it alone for the moment.

A slim, tiny woman crept out from behind a bulky, brawny man. "His smell, it's odd. I smell Caris. But something else. He's not a Firewalker. But he's not human, either."

Sage's laughter filled the room, echoed by a deep sigh that came from Caris. "The cat's out of the bag," Sage said dryly.

The small woman flashed Sage a dark look and Jax noticed something odd about her eyes. Her pupils were almost elliptical, like, well, a cat's. Through another's mind, he did not know whose, he saw the woman stalking through the streets in silence, making no sound, leaping out of the shadows like a panther taking down prey. She hunted like a great cat, and this shamed her. She had fantastic night sight, an incredible sense of smell, and she hated herself. She wore gloves on her hands, except when prowling, for her hands had claws, much like his own fangs. They were retracted, unless she was hungry or angry.

Right now she was both.

She was also in heat.

Poor thing. A burning, aching mass of sexual frustration, and so full of need.

But she was focused on having a man she didn't think she could have, so she suffered through it.

The brawny man was her brother, her twin, actually, though obviously not identical. Big and broad, with anger burning in the depths of his green eyes, his shaggy blond hair spilling over his forehead, he was a vibrating pillar of rage to Jax's psychic senses.

He moved away from the small woman and glared at Sage—obviously these three were used to being at odds. The man towered nearly a head taller than Jax, and Jax was easily one of the tallest in the room. This man must be a giant among mortals. "What are you?" he grumbled, his voice deep and throbbing.

Caris moved in front of him and said, "That's really not today's issue, is it? I swear it, on my own soul, he can be trusted."

Morgan smiled, sardonically. "It's not that easy, sweet. You cannot so easily bring a stranger among us. If he were one of us, it would be acceptable—not wise, without first consulting me—but acceptable. He is not one of us. And Anni says he's not even human," Morgan said, eyeing Jax with unreadable eyes.

Jax moved to Caris' side, feeling her heat, reveling in it. He was willing to do what she suggested.

He wasn't expecting the suggestion that came, or who it came from.

I trust you, Sugar. Don't know him, but I trust you. If he wants to bare his soul, he can. If it goes bad, I'll get you both out of here. Morgan will calm down, and when he does, I'll let you know.

Caris' eyelashes barely flickered. She had heard Sage's whispered words as well. But no one else had. *Can I trust him?* he asked her.

Yes. He's a pain in the ass, but he is my best friend. He'd never betray me.

He lifted his eyes to Sage and studied the bland hazel gaze that watched him closely. *I hope you mean what you say, human. I do not think you are prepared for what I have to show you,* he warned.

Sage's lashes lowered slowly, a ghost of a smile hovering around his mouth. *She's not the kind of person you can fool, pretty boy. No matter who or what you are. If she trusts you, then you are trustworthy. I know that. They ought to. Just stay close. If this goes bad, I don't want to have to waste time going after two separate bodies. Keep a hold on her.*

Jax wrapped one brawny forearm around Caris' slim waist and held her close as he lifted his eyes to Morgan's. The man was waiting impatiently. He knew some silent communication was going on. "Caris, be careful what you do here," Morgan said.

"Be careful what you make me do here," she replied, wrapping her fingers around Jax's forearm. "I've been waiting my whole life for this man. I am not letting him go. Not for any reason. Our fight will continue, with or without me. I won't let you force me into giving up something I need."

The underlying deep throbbing intensity of her voice had the others around them shifting their feet, moving restlessly in their seats and Morgan's eyes narrowed. "Fuck it, Caris. You dreamed him?"

"He exists, Morgan. He just didn't exist in our dimension," she snapped, cuddling back into Jax. He rubbed his chin against her hair, staring hard at the man who advanced on them.

"How do you know?"

"I'm not powerful enough to create a man out of nothing," she scoffed. "I'm not God. For crying out loud, Morgan. Be realistic."

"I am being realistic. Your gift is unique, like nothing anybody has ever seen. How do we know—"

Jax interrupted quietly, "I know. I existed long before she pulled me out of my world and into yours. And I imagine it's not actually another dimension, just a different galaxy, one very, very distant from yours." He frowned, sliding Caris a look. "If I could study some charts, I perhaps could even discover where I am in relation to where I was." Then he drew one finger down her cheek. "Not that it matters. I will never leave your side."

"Oh, wonderful. A fucking spaceman," the brawny man drawled, shaking his shaggy head.

Jax choked off a laugh. "Not a spaceman," he said, tucking his tongue into his cheek.

"Then exactly what are you?" Morgan demanded. "You look human. But Anni is right. You do not feel human."

Jax let his fangs drop, letting the rage he always had to battle uncoil just a little. His eyes were glowing when he opened them to stare at Morgan and he whispered roughly, "Take a guess."

Chapter Five

Caris knew she had friends among the Firewalkers, just as she knew Morgan would be angry when she brought an Outsider in without his express consent. He wouldn't have given it.

She hadn't been surprised when Sage had offered his help.

But the aid of another surprised her.

Miguel moved out of the doorway where he had been watching all in silence. He had erected one of his barriers between Morgan and herself before Sage even had time to decide whether or not things were going badly. They hadn't—exactly. At least not yet.

But Dustin was getting ready to force the issue, his mind already made up as the others grappled with what they were seeing.

The others were still trying to adjust to the fact that her lover had suddenly developed inch-long fangs and eyes that glowed and swirled and hypnotized. Miguel stood just inches from her side, one hand out, fingers spread, the solidifying, shifting, swirling barrier keeping Dustin from seizing Jax. That was Dustin's first instinct against a threat, and why Sage had offered to get them out.

"He's not a threat to her or us, Dustin. Throttle down, buddy," Miguel said quietly. Once the barrier was solid, his dusky hand dropped to his side and he slid Caris an amused look. "You always manage to do the damnedest things to liven up a party, *chica.*"

She smiled tightly. "I wasn't trying, honest."

He brushed his hair out of his eyes and met Morgan's angry glare through the barrier. "What are you doing, Miguel?" he snarled.

"Giving the man a chance, Morgan, just like you gave us. Dustin's going into berzerker mode as we speak—" he glanced at the man built like a mountain who was pacing and clenching his ham-sized fists, shooting Miguel angry, darting venomous looks, "and we both know that if Dustin attacks, her friend is going to defend himself. What if he starts beating Dustin? Not an unlikely thing. Are you going to stand by and watch? So, I'm giving him a chance, without Dustin's temper getting the better of him."

Dustin snarled, "Did you see those fucking teeth?"

To their surprise, it was Anni who said quietly, silkily, "Dustin, haven't you seen mine?" She flashed her baby fangs at them and moved up to the barrier, studying Jax intently. "I've never seen another predator on two legs before. But I know when I've run into one stronger than me. Exactly what are you?"

"A vampire," he said softly.

There was silence in the room.

Disbelief.

Caris had expected laughter.

But Jax didn't compel that. Nothing about him compelled anybody to believe anything except that he was telling the truth. They may not trust him, they may fear him. But every last one of them believed him, whether they wanted to or not.

"Vampires don't exist," Dustin said roughly, curling his fingers over his sister's tiny shoulders. His hands looked massive on her slender frame. She reached up and laid one hand on his, holding it there, but she wouldn't back away as he wanted her to.

Jax lifted his eyes to the man who towered nearly a head above him and smiled slowly, letting him see the ivory teeth. "Perhaps not on your world, but they do on mine."

"How did you come to be here?" Anni asked, cocking her head and studying him intently, fascinated. Another predator...the words repeated in her mind, and Jax had an inkling of just how alone she'd felt, how much a freak.

"Caris brought me here." Lowering his head, he whispered against her neck, "Thank the Father—what did I do to deserve such a gift?"

"There are more like you?" Morgan asked tightly.

"Not here. But on my world? Many thousands, although we are slowly dying off. We are much feared, much hated in many parts. We've been repressed for the past ten centuries and our numbers are dying off. We cannot mate without permission, and though we can easily father children among our race, it is not allowed. Our offspring are killed the moment it is discovered that the woman is breeding. I am alive only because my mother went into hiding. By the time I was discovered, I was already two, and by that time, it would have been murder, and thus not allowed."

"This is bullshit," Dustin snapped. "Vampires don't exist! Not here, not on Earth. That's a damned kid's story. Vampires are not real."

"But I am vampire, and I am quite real." He tossed his booted feet a quick glance and then looked at Dustin from under his lashes. "I am on your world, am I not? So I believe vampires exist on your world."

"The sun..." Anni cleared her voice. "I thought vampires had to sleep during the day."

Jax softened his voice. This woman may have the equipment to be a predator, but she was hardly meant to be one. "On my world, we must. But I think it is our suns. We have two, and when they rise, they bring about a change in our bodies that makes us fall into a deep sleep, and the touch of it will burn our flesh. Another galaxy I have traveled has three and none of my kind dare go there. The sun here stings my skin some, and hurts my eyes, but I feel no danger from it."

"Blood?"

This came from Sage.

"My life source," he responded. "But while I am not ancient, I need little to maintain my strength. And it does not have to be human." Then he got nasty. "Unless of course you want to donate. But I do not like men."

Sage sneered at him. "Caris?" He cocked a brow.

She ignored him. He moved in her direction but Jax felt the mental command she sent to Sage. *Don't. That won't help and he hasn't done anything I haven't wanted and downright begged for,* she insisted, keeping her eyes focused on the people in front of them.

"Why are you feared?" Morgan asked coldly. He ignored everybody but Jax. He was certain of everybody but the vampire. Even Caris. Even if she walked away with the vampire, she was no threat to him, and she would help him every time he called on him. Sage was his—he was loyal to Morgan to his death, Miguel, Dustin, Anni, all of them.

But the vampire, he was an unknown.

Jax cocked his head and asked quietly, "Why are you? You are hated by your neighbors, your brothers, your friends. You meet in secret. And for the same reasons as I. Your young are killed in infancy by their own kind, something even my world has not yet stooped to. We are different, that is why I am feared on my homeworld, why you are feared on yours.

"I am not like them. I can read their minds without even trying. I am ten times stronger than their strongest warrior." He glanced at Dustin and smiled insolently. "As strong as your mountain looks there, I wager I could take him to the ground and turn this room red with his blood, had he laid one hand on me. If I had so desired it. I would not have. I would not harm the friends of my woman. But it is within my ability. I need only feed every few days. I can take more pain than your mind can possibly comprehend. I can coerce the minds of those who are not gifted with powers like mine, or Caris, or Sage. In my world, vampires live for one thousand years or longer, but I do not know if our years are the same as yours. I can run tirelessly, fight endlessly, move quicker than your mortal eyes can track.

"At one time, my kind had enslaved the people of Oslina. For more than ten thousand years, they were our slaves, and we the masters. Eventually, we were overthrown. Our weaknesses, though few, are grievous and the mortals learned quickly how to exploit them. The wars took more than a thousand years, but for the past ten centuries, the mortals have ruled, and they have tightened their grip to where we are little more than dogs."

"You don't look too submissive to me," Morgan stated flatly.

"A vampire is a predator," Jax said, struggling to reign in his anger. "A hunter. But in order to live, we must control that. Do you know how humiliating it is to beg permission to buy your own home? If I had ever taken a mate, I would have had to plead my case before the King. I would never have been allowed to father a child. I cannot feed on a mortal without requesting permission, even from those who set themselves up merely for that trade. The blood-whores love nothing more than to find a wealthy vampire and cry he blood-raped her, when he courted and requested permission in truth. We are dominant creatures, but if we dare to allow that to show, we are put to death. They are destroying us. Within a few more millennia, we will all be gone."

"How sad," Dustin mocked lightly. "The poor traumatized vampires are being hunted to extinction."

Jax flashed fang. "I'd be careful, mountain," he whispered silkily. "What do you think your own people are doing to you? At least the people exterminating my kind are not my own blood."

Before Dustin could hurl himself at Miguel's unbreakable barrier, Morgan stepped between them and said quietly, "He is right, Dustin. Damn it, why do you think they are killing the babies? Hunting down the kids? We are being exterminated. Hearing it put so bluntly doesn't change anything."

"My kind at least have time on their side. They will fight back, eventually. They already know what is to come," Jax said, shoving his own grief down. Faraman had spoken to him in quiet tones, in hushed voices, about the vampire revolts taking place throughout Oslina. But Jax had not wanted to stage one, lead one or participate in one. Faraman may have felt it was the only way, and Jax knew in his gut it was not right to cow a man so, be he mortal or vampire, but he would not harm his King. "But yours has not. You are divided, and poorly organized, and too full of anger."

"We have reason to be angry," Morgan whispered roughly. "They kill us, in our cribs. Some of our brothers have died at the hands of their parents. They attack us in the night, shoot us in the back. We have every right to be angry."

"Your anger will not save you if you let it blind you," Jax said softly. "When I was twenty, the King I serve tried to make me a eunuch. He tried to convince me that was for the good of the world. I could have fought and killed the men he sent for me, but where would my anger have gotten me? Dead. Thrown to the suns or beheaded. Anger does you little good if you cannot control it."

He felt the shudder that racked Caris and he held her tighter, stroking one hand up and down her arm as he stared into Morgan's eyes. "I am no threat to you."

"You are too alien." Morgan shook his head, his glistening hair flowing around his wide shoulders, his pale blue eyes troubled. "Caris, we need you, but I can't have this man here."

"Then I'm not here either," she said quietly. "I'll try to help the boy Sage mentioned, but then I'll have Sage take me home." Reaching up, she closed her hand around the charm at her neck and started to tug.

"Caris, no," Anni said, a soft whimper in her throat. She turned tearful eyes to Morgan, her dark, stormy gray gaze glittering. "Why are you so willing to turn him aside?

Damn it, it was just a few years ago that I killed men in cold blood when the hunger was on me. After I hit puberty, it took you months to bring me under control. I killed innocent men, and you still kept me on. Why me and not him?"

"You were a child. And damn it, he's not one of us," Morgan snarled, flinging a hand in Jax's direction. His hand struck Miguel's barrier and he bellowed as the electrical shock tore through him. Cradling his injured hand to his chest, he fell away and brushed aside Dustin's aid. "He's not one of us."

"Hypocrite," Sage said quietly. He ignored Morgan's angry, outraged eyes and turned to Caris with a look she rarely saw. Compassion. He had so much rage inside him, compassion was something he just didn't have much room for. "I'll bring the boy out." He was gone, and back within seconds, holding the child cuddled against his chest.

The boy was pale, wide-eyed, the dark brown irises huge in his small face. Caris started to smile but an odd tingle raced down her spine as she stared at his sweet, young face. *Foul...perverted...they should die...* Not thoughts she was sensing from him, those were muffled, shielded.

But emotions...foul, evil...

Warily, she reached out but jerked her hand back. "Has any other empath been here to see him?"

Angrily, across the barrier, Morgan snarled, "No. I wanted you here for him. None of the others are like you. Even Ari and Kelly can't touch your skill, though I tried to summon a healer as well as you. I wanted the best I had for a child. But you don't have a care for us any longer."

She ignored him. Morgan would not stay so angry with her for long. He needed her too much. His temper ran as hot as his gifts did, and tended to burn out just as quickly. Flatly, she said, "The boy isn't in here, Morgan. The boy isn't inside this body. And you all need to get out of here. Now. Sage."

Sage didn't question. Miguel remained holding the barrier, but Sage crossed it, grabbed Anni and they were gone.

"What?" Morgan asked, pacing, his entire being wanted to be by the child. And his anger kept him away. Miguel wouldn't drop the barrier while Dustin was there, reacting to every little nuance from his leader.

Miguel, the stubborn bastard, took his responsibilities seriously, and had decided that he'd be on Caris' side. Flinging himself into a chair, he brooded.

Jax knelt beside her and studied the boy. "Father of us all," he whispered under his breath. "How is that possible?" He could see the face inside the body. It was not that of a child. It was watching and listening. "Could he hear us from where he was?"

"No. Morgan keeps the children in an old room in the basement. It was built hundreds of years ago, called a bomb shelter. But him hearing us doesn't matter. They are tracking him somehow. Using him as a beacon. They are on their way here now."

Morgan had risen and was watching them through the barrier. "What's going on?" he asked as he picked up on the nuances he saw on Caris' face.

"No time," Sage said as he exploded back into the room. "Something bad is coming. I feel it now." His tanned face was lined from weariness as he strode to

Dustin, looped his arms as best he could around the man's massive girth, and they were gone.

"Damn it, Caris."

"No questions, Morgan, it's not safe." She closed her hands around the tiny face that looked so innocent. The soul inside it was not. It was full of malice and evil and cunning. It was so certain it had won. "Not so easy, bastard," she snarled into his face.

"Let me," Jax murmured. "I think I can do something about this."

He laid his long fingered hands along the back of hers as Sage exploded, with a little less oomph into the room, and strode to Morgan. Morgan shook his head. "I'm last," he said. "My agents go first. Their safety first."

Miguel cocked a black brow. His Hispanic features softened with a smile as he asked, "*Amigo*, you going to play nice?"

"I'll play nice, Miguel," Morgan said flatly, his blue eyes gleaming.

The barrier fell, Sage gripped Miguel and then there were four, Morgan, Caris, the boy and the vampire. "He's trying to track Sage. I can place a mental block," Jax murmured, weaving it as he spoke. He opened his eyes as he spoke and purred into the watcher's mind, *You chose a bad time to come. A mental predator is in the midst and I am so much harder to fool than they are. So much older.*

What are you doing? Get out get out get out get out get out get out! the shrill voice echoed throughout the room and even Morgan heard it.

Slowly he said, "That is no child."

Sage stumbled into the room this time. "Come on, Morgan." There was none of his characteristic cockiness, none of his natural grace, just an obvious weariness.

"Caris, first."

"No, man. She won't go without the vampire and he has to go last. He's keeping that boy from tracking, so he stays until I'm done. No arguing, I ain't got the energy," Sage said. He looped his arms over Morgan.

Within seconds, he was back again and drawing her against him, a reassuring smile on his face. "Come on, Sugar. Let's go," he said, nodding at the vampire. "I'll be back."

Caris knew it would be bad. The jaunt with Sage was beyond bad. Her belly was roiling with it. But she stumbled and fell and managed to keep from hitting her head just barely. She stumbled out of the way just as Sage reappeared with the boy who wasn't a boy. She jerked her feet away from him, not wanting to touch him. She needed another teleporter—Sage's weariness was far too great and he was pushing himself too hard.

But there was not enough time.

Sage appeared with Jax and collapsed against the vampire, gray, his eyes rolling upward until only the whites showed. Jax caught him and held him easily, gently. "As he came back the last time, something was surrounding the house. Very loud. Very fast. I hope nothing of importance was there," Jax murmured as he eased him onto the couch so she could look at him.

Caris heard and felt the broadcast call from another agent go up thirty minutes later as she watched Jax slip Sage's limp body into her bed. The vampire had stripped him down and she had examined him, pressing the pads of her fingers to his brow and tunneling into his mind.

"Exhaustion, overuse. He's going to have the granddaddy of all headaches. And he most likely will be earthbound and walking where he wants to go for a week, at least," she told Morgan who stood silently in the doorway, watching them with grim eyes. "You're gonna hate that, aren't you, babe?" she murmured, stroking his black hair back from his face.

The boy was still where they'd left him. Jax checked on him periodically.

MORGAN!!!! The sheer panicked pain in that voice was unrecognizable. Not a voice she could ever remember hearing. But when it calmed a few heartbeats later and touched her again, it sounded more familiar. Vaguely.

Caris? Caris! Of course, calm was a relative term. The powerful voice was still enough to shatter, or at least feel like it was shattering, her eardrums.

She clapped her hands instinctively over her ears, even though the sound didn't come from outside her head, but from within.

Pipe down. I'm here. Who is this?

Where's Morgan? His house is gone, totally. Where is he?

With me. We got out. Who is this?

Oh, sorry. Ari Rayborne. Where is Morgan, damn it? Where is here?

Rayborne. That explained the powerful call.

He is here. He's fine.

She lifted her eyes and stared at Morgan in the doorway. "The house is gone."

Call everybody you can find. We need to meet, but no teleporting. They may have found a way to track us.

She had no more than relayed the message to the powerful telepath Ari when she felt another prodding at her shields. But this wasn't a telepath trying to get in. It was an empath–and if Caris didn't let her in, the empath would simply force her way inside. Caris knew who this was.

When Caris lowered her shields, the questions didn't come in words, but in emotions and feelings, pictures, not thoughts.

But Kelly Maguire's questions were clear enough. She wanted, needed, to know how Sage was.

Kelly, love, he is fine.

A more powerful urge overtook Caris' being, and she felt her throat tighten at the depth of the emotion. Tears stung her eyes and she had to take a deep, shaky breath before she could answer forcefully, *Kelly, throttle down...you're leaking all over me. And he is going to be fine. I know you can't feel him. He's out, unconscious. But he isn't dead. I swear it.*

The cloak of misery lifted slightly and Caris could breathe. *Honey, I know we haven't always gotten along well. We both are too close to Sage for that, but I don't lie. You know me. I don't lie.*

After long moments, a wave of relief passed and Caris wished she could just hug the younger woman. Kelly transmitted the feeling that she would be making her way to Montana as quickly as she could.

Go safely...

But the healer had already broken the link.

It figured. Nothing would keep Maguire from getting to the side of her beloved Sage.

Later that night, Caris lay her head on Jax's naked shoulder. The gel mat underneath them padded the floor and absorbed the cool from the early spring night so they were nearly as comfortable as they would have been in the bed.

She hadn't wanted to leave Sage alone just yet and all the guest suites were on the opposite side of the house. She had two spare rooms left, and the couch folded out into a bed. Right now, it housed Miguel. He was taking watchdog duty on their little POW who was ensconced in what had once been a wine cellar. At Morgan's request, several years ago, she had revamped it with a steel reinforced door, soundproofed it, fireproofed it, and basically "proofed" it against everything short of a laser-bomb.

Periodically, she sensed Miguel up and moving around down in the basement as he went to check on the not-child but other than that it was quiet.

They were expecting company, and lots of it, within the next few days.

They needed to find a new headquarters.

Her house was big, but not big enough for several hundred agents.

Hell, Morgan's house hadn't been big enough for that.

When will he wake?

When he wants to, **Caris** replied. *He just wore himself out, stretched himself too thin. He was teleporting us over a distance of nearly five hundred miles, one way. Other 'porters would never have been able to do that more than once. Sage is pretty powerful. We're lucky he didn't wipe himself out.*

The consequences of that tightened her throat and stung her eyes. Desperate to think of something else, Caris slid her hand down and closed it over his cock. *Think you could be quiet if I…?* She sent him a mental picture that had him arching off the gel mat, his body vibrating with a suppressed moan. A thrill of delight raced through her, and the lust and need chased away her grim thoughts as he wrapped one hand in her hair and urged her down.

Sliding under the thin sheet, she closed her mouth over the fat head of his cock and sucked on it like a lollipop, as his fingers tightened in her hair. His taste, damn, it was addictive. She curled her tongue around the plum-shaped head, sucking it hard and humming with pleasure as he groaned. He arched up against her mouth, taking the cue from her mind.

She could feel a battle waging inside him, the battle to be and act as he truly was, tempered with the self-imposed, rigid control he had always been forced to maintain.

His hands held her head, but almost tentatively, and she could feel the way he battled down the desire to grip her tightly, to drive roughly into her mouth until he exploded.

You're a dominant creature…I'm not submissive, but I don't mind being dominated every once in a while, she thought. She could never have said the words, or even thought the words outside of sex.

But she might have worked up the courage if she had realized just how badly he needed to hear them. She felt something inside him break, the final chains he had been keeping in place after so many years of suppressing his own nature. He pulled away from her, rolled to his knees and pulled her to hers before grabbing her head and twining her long hair around his fingers, urging her mouth to his rampant erection. The need for silence made it all the more erotic as he thrust his thick length past the barrier of her lips and teeth, the glans of his cock bumping the back of her throat. As he slid down and down while he meshed with her mind, he whispered, *relax, relax, relax,* and she actually felt him take over her body, forcing the muscles to relax until she had taken as much of his length inside her throat as she could, and still be able to breathe.

He wrapped one hand around his length to mark her limit and started to shuttle back and forth, ordering her silently, *Hold still,* when she started to draw back. *Ah, damn it, you have no idea how sweet you look.* Her jaws ached, her mouth actually felt bruised from his width as he drove his cock back inside, a muffled groan falling from his lips this time.

Caris felt his grip in her hair fall away as he trailed his hand down her back. He gripped her ass, stroking the firm round curve, tracing his finger down the crevice there and asking, *Has this tiny little hole ever taken a man's cock?*

No, she thought in shock at the foreign caress. Hot little jolts of sensation coursed through her at the thought.

"Good," Jax purred out loud, keeping his voice quiet. He brought one hand to his mouth and licked his fingers until they gleamed. Then he started to press against that rosy, puckered hole, smiling as she whimpered around his cock. He pushed a little harder into her mouth and shuddered when the muscles in her throat closed silkily over him as they tried instinctively to reject him.

The little rosette was tiny, virgin and tight. He bore down relentlessly until, with a sob, she opened around him and he worked his finger inside. Once in to the knuckle, he held still and reached up with his other hand to support her head, thrusting deeply inside her mouth, staring down at her. With his acute vision, he could see easily.

He also knew Sage had been awake for the past several minutes, and the mortal was watching them, with sleep-heavy, hungry eyes. Jax did not particularly care. His heart was racing and the scent of the man's arousal was filling the air, mingling with their own as he stared, watching Caris deep-throat Jax's cock, a hungry little moan falling from her. Watching Jax finger-fuck Caris' virgin ass.

Never would he let her be with another man, alone. But if Jax let another man share in her sweetness, the pleasure she could derive from that...

With a hoarse groan, he shuddered as the tight muscles in her ass clamped around his finger and he pulled it out slightly before working it back in. Her sweet, hot mouth slid back down on his cock and then she closed a firm, gentle hand over his sac, pressing the pads of her fingers against the sensitive patch of flesh right behind his balls.

Her hot, silky-wet tongue stroked over the rigid erection and Jax's breath left him in a rush as he pushed his cock deeper into her mouth, feeling her throat close over him, resisting, the muscles caressing the head of his shaft teasingly.

His climax was building at the base of his spine and he wasn't certain he wanted to go over the edge without her, but he wasn't relinquishing his position in her mouth either.

"What kind of fantasies have you had, Caris?" he asked huskily as he started to plunge his finger inside her ass. "This, I know. I see it inside your mind. What else? Tell me what I have glimpsed in your heart, share them with me."

Too many to count. They flooded the link between them, hot, erotic pictures filling Jax's mind—the one he had glimpsed before was there, in full bright color. Complete, vivid, and something she'd never dare whisper of in the daylight.

"Sweet thing," Jax purred as he singled that particular fantasy out and focused on it. "You've dreamed of being taken by two men at once, haven't you, love? Feeling the pleasure that brings..."

He lifted his eyes to Sage, who had slowly sat up. Sage was watching them with narrowed eyes but started to shake his head. "No way," he said hoarsely. But he continued to stare down at them.

Caris jerked up, pulled her mouth from Jax's rigid cock, and fell against the vampire, staring at Sage with wide, shocked eyes. Embarrassment stained her cheeks red. Through the windows positioned behind and over the bed, moonlight poured in, enough for them to see each other clearly, and Sage had been her lover long enough to recognize the shocked, startled arousal in her eyes.

"Fuck," he muttered, shaking his head. He slid from the bed and crawled to them, staring at her face, as if to make sure he had seen what he had thought he had seen. It was there. The need, the desire. "Every damn one of them are gonna hear us." He slid one hand up her slim thigh and brushed his thumb against her wet slit, found her swollen clit and started to circle it with firm, certain strokes as he lowered his head to catch one rock-hard nipple in his mouth.

Jax rocked his cock against her backside, gripping her hips with his hands, as he whispered into her mind, for her alone, *If you had taken a man into your ass before, that is what I would be doing now. But it is good you have not. I want that pleasure to be mine. Only mine.* His voice dropped to a rough purr that seemed to caress her from the inside out as his other hand went around to cup the breast that Sage was not sucking on. *I will settle for driving my cock down your throat tonight, while he fucks you. And when I have you ready, I will slide my cock inside your ass. Would you like to have two men at once, feeling him deep inside your pussy while I fuck that sweet ass of yours?*

"Yes," she whimpered, tossing her head back and forth. Sage's teeth scraped her nipple roughly as he worked two fingers inside her slippery wet sheath. She sobbed and thrust her hips against him, riding his hand hungrily.

Sweet girl, Jax murmured, stroking her hair. He shifted and moved, urging her onto her hands and knees as Sage settled back onto his knees. The human male was shaking his head, rubbing his temple blearily and muttering, "I don't think the doctor said, take three and call me in the morning. Could be wrong."

Jax groaned as Caris again eagerly closed her mouth over his cock. Her position opened her wet folds and Sage swore gruffly and hunkered over her, taking his cock in hand and driving roughly inside her. He gripped her hips and worked his length deep inside the already convulsing, silky sheath of her pussy. He slid one hand under her and caught her clit, pinching it lightly at first, then more roughly as she started to press her hips greedily against his hand.

"So damn hot," Sage rasped. "You're gonna burn me alive." He groaned as she vised down around his cock, while Jax wrapped his hands in her hair and held her head still as he forced his length slowly, firmly inside her mouth. *Open, open, sweet, damn it, damn it, you are sweet*, he rasped inside her mind.

Caris was dying. Sage drove his burning hot cock completely inside her while his rough, calloused fingers played their magic on her clit. And Jax—he was forcing his cock inside her mouth, past her throat, robbing her of the ability to breathe, to think, while he crooned praises and pleas in her mind, as he held her by the hair.

She jerked and sobbed as Sage plucked at her clit as he withdrew, then pushed slowly back inside, his throbbing length rasping over her G-spot. Over and over, until her body was tight and shaking with the need to come.

The climax was coiling tight in her belly. It was going to break over her and she couldn't stop it. She pumped her head furiously, slurping and suckling on Jax's cock hungrily, craving the alien, almost sweet taste of his skin. The taste of his skin wasn't like that of a human man, but different, odd, unique, mellow, sweet, hot.

Behind her, she heard Sage as he growled, shoved her hips lower, drove harder inside her, his cock jerking as he came, his semen hot, pulsating and rolling against her womb as it jetted from him. It set off her orgasm. She felt it start and she couldn't stop the scream that built in her throat around Jax's cock. He did, though, gripping her head and forcing his length farther down as he started to pulse and come in her throat. Groaning raggedly, pumping his hips in tiny, rapid little circles against her mouth, he emptied himself.

"Oh fuck," Sage groaned long moments later.

Sage felt the vampire's eyes on him over the length of Caris' still quivering body. His body was shaking, he was sweating and dizzy, and he was pretty certain his head was going to split into at least two different pieces, maybe three.

"You all right?" she managed to gasp out. Then she giggled. "Little late to ask, though."

"Fucking trying to kill me. I'm the walking wounded." Sage's voice was a rough, gravelly rumble in the quiet room, but the pitiful words were ruined by the snicker he couldn't quite suppress.

Sage rarely snickered.

"You could have done the polite thing," she said as she tried to catch her breath. "Pretended to sleep."

"What fun would that have been?" He flopped onto his belly and grunted. "Take the damn bed. Ain't no way I can get up there," he muttered.

Jax laughed. He stood and tossed Caris' giggling body onto the bed. Then he took Sage's swearing one and did the same, onto the far side of the mammoth, lake-sized bed. "I would dare say, after that, there is no reason for any of us to sleep on the floor, Sage," he said, crawling into the bed, cuddling against Caris. "Especially considering that I plan on enjoying that again." He slid into sleep moments later, feeling her arm slide around his waist.

Caris awoke less than two hours later. Her body was pleasantly sated, with the sweet ache of sex riding it, her mind blurred by exhaustion, and she should have been able to sleep.

But no dice.

She slid down to the foot of the bed as silently as she could. Not quite enough, she knew. *Where are you going?* Jax opened his eyes, gazing at her from under his lashes. The cloudy feel of his thoughts told her how very tired he was.

Sage slept on, truly like the dead this time, she knew by a light touch to his mind. "I can't sleep. I have insomnia." She didn't waste the words to explain, just shot him the mental picture and felt his understanding. "Go back to sleep. You're tired, as well. I'm going to take a bath and then I'll try to sleep a little more. But if I get to talking and thinking, I won't sleep at all."

As Caris ran the bath, she offered a silent apology if she was disturbing anybody. Tossing in lavender bath salts, she also decided to dump in some vanilla oils, just because she liked to the way the two scents mingled together on her skin. After she clipped her hair up on her head Caris slid into the tub, blanking her mind.

This was all old hat to her. Many, many nights had been spent this way. Well, she thought with a smug, hot little smile, not exactly this way. She couldn't believe what Jax had done. What Sage had done.

What she had let them do.

Damn it.

Just the thought made her belly quiver, brought a rush of wet heat to her cleft and had her breath shuddering out of her in a hungry sigh.

A fantasy, so long kept hidden, and now it had happened. Jax had known, and he had given it to her. And planned on doing it again…his words still lingered in her mind, the words he had whispered as she was sliding into sleep, cradled between Jax and Sage.

She reached for the thick specially imported sponge. Americans rarely indulged in some of the more basic pleasures these days. Bathing, to her fellow countrymen, was a chore to be dealt with quickly and with as little mess as possible. Caris loved baths, long and hot, with scented, oiled water soaking and softening her skin. She loved that the money her parents had left her allowed her to indulge in some of her more enjoyable little fetishes.

Like the sea sponge. She lazily scrubbed her arms and chest and belly, then her legs before tossing it aside. Poor Anni, the girl had never taken a real bath before coming here with Caris a few years ago. She had dropped down into the deep, custom-made tub with a sigh of pure bliss.

Eventually, the water, the heat, the scent of the lavender worked their magic and Caris knew she could retreat back into sleep. The niggling little doubts that had awoken her never sprang to the forefront of her mind, so whatever the trouble, it wasn't dire. So she could sleep.

She snuggled down between the warm, heavy male bodies with a cat's smile. She knew she couldn't have this for too damn long, but damn, while she could...

Caris awoke to feel Jax's tongue and teeth on her clit. He screwed two thick fingers in and out of her wet passage while she moaned her way into wakefulness. Her lashes lifted and she stared down her body to see him watching her closely, hungrily. She jumped when Sage whispered against her ear, "Hot, sleepy woman. Nothing better to wake up to." His hand smoothed over her belly, up her torso to close on her breast, pinching her already peaked nipple just before his head swooped down, and his hot mouth fastened on it. "Unless it's followed by fucking you again. Damn, you taste sweet."

Whimpering, she rocked her hips upward as Jax moved lower, and started to thrust his tongue inside her. Her eyes crossed, and she swore every last nerve ending inside her vagina exploded as his big hands closed over her ass and held her still. He kept the stabbing motion up until she was sobbing and coming against his mouth. Sage covered her mouth with his and swallowed the scream before she could wake everybody in the house.

Caris was still shaking when she was rolled onto her knees. Only the strength of Jax's hands held her up as he started to work his way inside the swollen tissues of her pussy. Sage cupped her head in his hands, staring down at her hungrily, his eyes narrowed to thin slits, his mouth grim, his face stark with hunger. He brushed her tangled, damp hair away from her face before rubbing his thumb across her lower lip.

"Open your pretty mouth, Sugar. Let me in," he purred.

She couldn't believe the slow, hot smile that uncurled across his face. She slid her eyes from his, down Sage's lean muscled body, while behind her, Jax shuttled his thick, long cock in and out in a slow, deep rhythm, his hands gripping her hips and holding her steady for the powerful thrusts of his hips. Caris lowered her head and stuck out her tongue, licked up the length of Sage's cock before lifting her eyes back up to his.

"Tease," he growled out.

She laughed before lowering her head again and taking him completely in her mouth, falling into a steady, shallow rhythm. He hadn't bathed after he had fucked her last night, and she could taste her cream that had dried on him, and his own semen. She licked and suckled on his cock until he was clean, then she licked some more, pushing her ass harder back against Jax.

He was hard, hot, pulsing within her like nothing she had ever felt, rubbing over her G-spot as he growled, hunkering lower over her body and driving harder into her, until she was gasping around Sage's cock from the force of the thrusts. Sage buried his hands in her hair and started to pump his length back and forth between her lips, staring down at her, lips open, eyes half blind with lust, sweat beading and rolling down his tanned face. The muscles in his belly clenched and bunched as he fucked his cock in and out of her swollen, pink mouth.

"Damn, that's a pretty sight," Sage teased. "Harder, baby, suck harder."

Caris whimpered when Jax reached around and caught her clit, pinching it roughly. Then he pushed even harder into her, making her writhe around him. She shoved back against him, then jerked when he slapped the smooth, rounded flesh of her ass. Freezing, she caught her breath, the action seeming to draw Sage even deeper. His hands clenched tightly on her head and he started to come, biting down on his lip to muffle the long, ragged groan.

Jax had slapped her soft, white ass without even thinking, but he felt the hot waves of lust rolling off of her, and tasted them, they were like some sweet, exotic rich wine. He applied his hand again with stinging force and she shuddered, clenched around him like some silken little vise, and started to come.

He pummeled his aching cock into the soft, silky depths of her convulsing pussy, growling as she shuddered and came, spasming around him with a grip that was so fucking tight, he thought his cock was going to explode inside of her.

Caris rocked back against him, wiggling her tight little butt, sucking hungrily on Sage's cock, slurping the last little drops of semen from him before letting him pull away from her. Jax pumped into her, hard and rough, three deep driving times, while she quaked and shivered and sobbed her way through climax, biting her forearm to muffle her scream.

She collapsed, ended with her head on Sage's thigh as Jax pulled his cock from her cleft with a wet sucking sound. He sat at her hip, smoothing his hand up and down her ass, staring down at her with hot, possessive eyes.

She smiled sleepily at him and didn't even realize it when she slid back into sleep.

Sage brushed her tangled hair away, automatically reaching down and stroking the muscles of her neck and shoulders, guiding her further into sleep. He met Jax's eyes levelly. "I'm not in love with her," he said softly. "She's important to me. And I'll kill you if you hurt her. But I don't have any plans to try messing things up for her, or you. She's happy." His hazel eyes dropped to study her sleeping face. They softened with a smile as he studied her. "Caris hasn't been happy for a long time."

"Why has she not?" Jax asked.

Sage settled back against the headboard, frowning. "I probably shouldn't be the one telling you. She won't. And as sweet and innocent as she looks, Caris is not somebody you want mad at you. But, well, her gifts…she's afraid of them. She doesn't let herself want things, doesn't let herself need things, or wish for things." Then he lifted one muscled shoulder with a wry grin. "Of course, maybe if she had…" His voice trailed off as he slid Jax a look. "After all, look where you ended up. And there's more, about why she can't let herself feel too much. But that is for her to explain. But it's dangerous for her to expose herself too much."

He carefully slid his leg out from under her. "She needs to sleep. She hasn't been sleeping well again. But it would be a good idea for you to wait in here a while," he suggested pointedly.

"And that is because...?"

Sage snagged his clothes on his way to the bathroom. "That's because I know the guys out there. You don't. If they're gonna be jackasses, I'm more equipped to handle them before they say something that's gonna end up pissing you off enough to hurt 'em. Or before they can do or say something that could hurt her."

Chapter Six

The only one with anything to say was Dustin.

And Sage wasn't surprised.

Dustin had been obsessed with Caris for years. Caris knew, but she avoided it. The fact that Sage was sleeping with her was a sore spot for Dustin. That Caris was sleeping with this fucking new freak was not a sore spot, it was a bullet wound. But Dustin hadn't just heard them last night. He hadn't just listened and stewed and brooded.

He had planned on barging in.

If Miguel hadn't literally stopped him, he would have kicked the door down, and Sage had no doubt blood would have flowed.

So Sage had his hands full.

He had wisely strolled outside under the pretense of needing some air to clear his aching head. It wasn't aching so much as just…muffled. No zipping around for him for a couple days, he mused as he leaned against the corral fence. The few horses in the corral tossed him a disinterested look and the two hired hands Caris kept around knew his face well enough that all they did was wave and go about their work.

He heard Dustin's solid footfalls and braced himself. There was no fucking way he was going to get into a fistfight with Dustin Michaels. The man could lift a bloody jetcar, he weighed 300 pounds, stood 6'9" and looked like…well, a mountain, as Jax had called him. Muscled, powerful, immovable.

But he was wrong.

"Have a nice night?" Dustin asked snidely.

Sage turned slowly and replied easily, "Slept good. Head hurts a little. Thanks for asking."

"It's bad enough you got to fuck her, knowing how much I want her, but do you have to let him do it at the same time?" he snarled, moving a menacing step closer. "Damn it, she's your girl and you shared her with him."

"Caris isn't my girl, never really has been. She's my friend, my lover from time to time, but I don't claim her any more than she claims me," Sage said tiredly, rubbing his neck.

"And that makes her fucking another man while you're there — worse — her fucking you both acceptable?"

Sage held his ground. He sure as hell couldn't teleport away. The odd, muffled feeling in his head was a sure sign he had drained those reserves dry and he would have to rest, rebuild them. And he couldn't fight Dustin. He had seen the mammoth man literally rip the arms off a government agent who had been trying to keep them from liberating a young Firewalker child by means of firepower. That sight hadn't rested well with Sage.

But he wasn't completely helpless. "What Caris does and doesn't do isn't your business, Dustin. She isn't interested in you — she made that clear a long time ago. Get over it, man."

"Get over it?" Dustin snarled, his face pale except for two flags of color high on his cheeks. "Get fucking over it? I had to listen while the woman I love let two men fuck her at once. You don't even love her! And the other one ain't even fucking human!" That wide barrel chest was letting out a booming, gravelly roar now and Sage knew it was only a matter of time before Morgan got out there. "I'm supposed to get over knowing she's turning into a fucking slut—"

"Watch it," Sage growled, his hazel eyes going cold and mean, his mouth firming down. His face went harsh and his hands flexed as rage spilled through him. The rage fueled him and hot little licks of power raced up and down his spine, firing his other gifts. "Be careful, Dustin. Be very, very careful of what you say from here on out. Nobody insults Caris like that, nobody."

Dustin sneered. "What you gonna do 'bout it, little man? You can't go flitting away like the coward you are, so what are you gonna do?" he mocked as he barreled at him.

One hand snapped up, palm out only microseconds before Dustin would have plowed into him. Dustin was grabbed, snapped into the air and held. A burning, searing jolt of pain ripped through Sage's head, sweat beaded on his lip. Distantly he heard the door to the house swing open, but he focused only on Dustin, on wrapping the invisible hands around him.

"You forgot, old pal, who helped teach Miguel, didn't you?" he whispered gruffly, as his body started to tremble from the strain. The more Dustin fought, the harder he had to struggle to hold him. If he hadn't been so fucking weak, it would have been nothing to hold the giant in the air indefinitely. Slowly, he closed his hand into a fist, and watched as Dustin's face paled while his air supply was cut off. "You forget, the teleporting is the gift I use the most. But it's not the only one. And it's not even the most powerful."

"What in the fuck is going on?" Morgan demanded as he strode from the house, his blue eyes snapping with anger, gleaming red so very faintly. His long, graceful body was tensed with rage as he stopped beside them, staring at Dustin with narrowed eyes. "Dustin, have you forgotten yourself again?"

"Fuck you both," Dustin gasped.

But his outrage was obliterated by the arrival of Jax. He came striding up, his eyes glowing, his fangs dropped, fury written in every line of his body.

"Put the mountain down, Sage, before you collapse," the vampire said quietly. "You weakened yourself far too much, saving us all on the yestereve."

"Might not be the wisest thing," Sage said, even though his voice was starting to wobble and the pain was starting to blind him. "Dusty here wants blood."

"Then he shall have it," Jax promised seductively, his voice low and silky.

Sage glanced at Jax warily.

The vampire smiled, a flash of teeth in his golden face. "Oh, do not worry. I shall not hurt him, much. But he called my lady a, ah, what was it? Yes, a slut. I do not believe I care for that word. We use a different one where I am from, but they all mean the same thing.

"He insulted her, questioned her honor, her heart, that is not something I can abide," he murmured as he stalked a tight circle around the man who still hung in midair, his face turning a pale blue now from lack of air, while Jax stared up at him.

"He is unable to breathe—a strange gift you have, Sage. And while I understand your fury, Caris is mine. He called my lady a slut. This is my insult to avenge."

Morgan's eyes narrowed. "Dustin, you stupid fool," he hissed. Then he looked at Sage and nodded. "He's asked for it. Let him go before you fucking kill yourself."

Sage didn't have a choice — five seconds after Morgan had finished speaking, he felt the last of his strength give. He collapsed. Again. The past few days were doing a number on his pride.

* * * * *

Anni sidestepped Dustin and knelt beside Sage, her fingers gently brushing his soaked hair from his gray face, tangling her fingers in the silky strands for a brief moment. Then she moved aside so Miguel could lift him. Her heart twisted at the lingering scents of sex on his body, even as the demon inside her turned the blood in her body to fire.

She paused by Dustin who was slowly sitting up, still glaring angrily at Sage, totally ignoring the man behind him. She knelt slowly, in front of her brother. "Why, Dusty?" she whispered. "Caris doesn't love you. She's never going to. But that doesn't make her a whore."

"Fucking two men does," he snarled.

Anni closed her eyes and hissed, flexing her small hands. She wanted to hit him. Why was he so fucking obsessed? She lifted her eyes to the vampire behind her brother. "He's a jackass, I know. And he's being mean right now because he's hurt. He's wrong, completely and totally. But he's the only family I've got left. He's not a bad guy, Jax," she said quietly.

He smiled, and Anni felt a shiver run down her spine, heat pooling in her belly and between her thighs. If Caris was a whore, then maybe so was she, lusting after a man who lay unconscious, and sexually attracted to the man she was permitting to hurt her brother. Even if the jerk deserved it. But that face, that mouth, damn it...and his voice, like whiskey.

"I meant what I said, little sister. I will not hurt him — much. But no man shall speak of my lady that way."

And Dustin was still glaring at Sage.

Like Sage was the threat.

Anni retreated into the house. She didn't want to see it. She was in her heart a predator, just like Jax. Dustin was going to have to learn who the dominant was, who Caris' heart and body belonged to, and he was going to have to respect it. But she didn't particularly want to see it.

So she'd help clean Sage's weary, wounded body and curl up next to him.

And wish it had been her with him last night.

But what else was new?

"Get up, mountain. I prefer my battles to be as fair as I can make them. Perhaps I should wear a blindfold. Or tie an arm behind my back," Jax mused as Dustin continued to rub his throat.

Jax leaned back against the fence, narrowing his eyes slightly against the brightness of the sun. The human was paying him no attention. None. As he pushed to his feet, Jax struck. He lashed out with one booted heel, took both of Dustin's feet from under him and watched as the mountain went down with a crash. He was back against the fence before Dustin had even struck the ground.

"I am not finished with you," Jax said quietly. "I care little that you are angry with Sage. And I have no sympathy for your hurt feelings. A man with honor does not speak so callously of a lady, one he says he cares for. You insulted Caris — for that I will bring you pain."

Dustin was still lying on his ass trying to figure out what happened. "Get up," Jax growled as his fangs dropped. Hunger was starting to gnaw at his belly and it would have been a pleasure to rip open a vein and feed until this pathetic mortal was weak and listless.

Dustin shot to his feet as Jax's words penetrated, fast for a man of his size, and he whirled to glare at Jax. "I'm gonna rip you apart."

Jax flashed his fangs and he whispered tauntingly, "Come and try."

Dustin rushed him and got the receiving end of a fist that felt like it was made of titanium. His nose was a well of pain, his eyes watered, blood flowed. Broken. Roaring, he lashed out with a fist the size of a ham, but Jax was no longer there. The hair on Dustin's neck prickled right before he felt his arm get wrenched behind his back as he was whirled and slammed into the corral fence. He was ripped from that, then slammed into the ground while he struggled like a child, helpless and weak.

Jax smelled the blood, male, flat, but blood all the same. Saliva pooled in his mouth and he swallowed, shoving Dustin harder into the dirt as he growled, "She's not for you. Even if I had never arrived here, she is not for you. But you will never speak so of her again.

"How can you claim to care for her? Love her, even? Yet speak of her so? What foolishness is this? Have you no honor? No pride?" Jax rasped against his ear.

Dustin bucked and Jax slid off, retreated a short distance and waited while Dustin got to his feet. He wobbled, pressing one hand to his nose. Jax sneered as Dustin lunged for him again. The humans seemed to move in slow motion compared to him. He was able to move a complete circle around Dustin by the time Dustin reached the spot where Jax had stood.

He drove a fist into the unprotected kidney area and kicked at Dustin's knee, before wrapping an arm around his neck, beating his blood lust into submission as he rode the bellowing man to the ground. "Shut your mouth, you fucking fool," he growled. He barreled into Dustin's mind, smashed down the feeble walls so many humans seemed to have, and just took over, forcing his very being into the other man's mind.

Dustin had no psychic skills, other than a mild sort of sensing that allowed him to know whether or not a person was a Firewalker, or in Jax's case, human. Smashing into his brain was like smashing an eggshell.

"She is mine. I am hers. You are nothing to her beyond friendship, but with your words you seek to kill even that," Jax snarled. "But if you cause her pain, I cause you pain. One more word from your thoughtless mouth and I will...kill...you." His voice dropped to a rough purr as he forced the picture into Dustin's mind of just how he intended to do it.

"A vampire is not a creature you want angry at you, Dustin Michaels. I could take your mind and own it, make it mine. Your anger makes you weak. I could force you to walk into the building there and hang yourself, or make you drive into the town and fling your body from one of your tall buildings and smash it into pieces. Or I could drain you dry and you could watch and not struggle at all." His voice dropped to a seductively silken purr as he added, "I could even make you beg for it. I could make you want it."

Jax rose off of Dustin, unable to stay so close to the blood that still flowed, the call of it humming under his skin. He hunkered on his heels beside Dustin as the man rolled over and scrambled back, fear finally saturating him and overwhelming his jealous rage. "But what I would do, Dustin, should you say one more thing against her, is just beat you into a bloody pulp." He stared at him, waited for Dustin's eyes to meet his and acknowledge him, then he rose and walked away.

He felt their eyes on him when he crossed the threshold.

Anni looked from Dustin, pushing himself up slowly and painfully in the corral yards away, to Jax. "You didn't feed," she said quietly, studying him with narrow eyes. She knew the signs of hunger, better than the others, since she suffered them herself.

He quirked an eyebrow at her. "If I feed now, I am likely to kill what I feed from, Anni. I am angry with your brother, but I do not wish to kill him." He slid his eyes to meet Morgan's and he said, "The mountain is not hurt too terribly. But you had best teach him to watch his tongue. He will not speak so of Caris. Ever." His voice dropped to a rough growl and his fangs dropped even further, protruding past his lower lip, his dark blue eyes glowing and hot in his rage.

Morgan inclined his head. "I can't control Dustin. But if he can't control his tongue, he isn't welcome. He will understand that, I'll make sure of it," Morgan said quietly. His pale ice-like eyes lingered on the fangs and he suggested, "Shouldn't you go ah...feed?"

Jax inhaled and forced the fangs to retract slightly. They wouldn't draw back into their sheaths completely until he had fed, but he could control it somewhat. "Do not worry, Morgan. I control my hunger, not the other way around. I also control my anger. Is Sage well—will he be well?"

Miguel lifted his head from where he was studying Sage. His thick, dense black curls fell into his eyes and he absently brushed them aside as he glanced at Jax. Sage lay unconscious on the couch. Nobody had wanted to wake Caris, because then they'd have to explain what had happened. "I think he will be. The best person to ask is Caris, and I can tell by looking at her she's exhausted—"

Jax crossed the room to kneel by Sage. "What exactly do you ask Caris? Is it a psychic thing for which you look?" He shuddered in the presence of such life, smelling the ebb and flow of it. His own heart rate kicked up, and he had to close his eyes and breathe. It had been too long since he had fed fully and well.

"Yeah," Miguel muttered, unaware of Jax's torment.

Anni wasn't though. She moved closer, unable to trust the big predator so easily. He was a noble man, from what she could tell. But nobility seemed to die easily. And he was so damned hungry. Sage was an easy target, and Miguel was so unaware. Morgan wasn't completely blind either, and he narrowed his eyes and moved closer as well.

Jax reached out, laid one finger on Sage's brow, right between the thick, shaggy eyebrows. Burning, slicing pain overwhelmed him for the briefest of seconds as he hissed and fought the instinctive knee-jerk reaction to pull away. "He is hurting," he whispered quietly. "I'm no empath— but Father of us all, the pain is enough to break him. Have you healers among you?"

Anni flicked Morgan a glance.

"Kelly Maguire is coming, and several of my agents have hooked up with her, despite her attempts to lose them. She's too valuable to travel alone and she's too upset right now to use caution. I believe Chantel is with her — she is a traditional healer, and Kelly is an empathic healer. They will be here tomorrow or the day after. But they are moving slowly, and using more conventional methods, since we don't know how exactly they are tracking the teleporters," Morgan said, still watching Jax the way you would watch a snake, eyes narrowed and watchful, wary.

"He needs a healer, just to ease the pain. It tears at him…he cannot heal without rest, but he cannot truly rest while this pain rides him."

"Medications?" Morgan suggested blandly, lifting a white brow.

Jax frowned, running the unfamiliar word through his mind. Medications…herbs. Then he nodded. "That would help, I believe." Miguel started to rise but a look from Morgan stopped him. Jax barely noticed, so focused was he on Sage. Anni left and returned a few minutes later. She knelt by the men, moving slowly, not meeting Jax's eyes, or even looking at him. She was going to have to trust Miguel and Morgan to protect Sage if Jax lost control — as a predator, she was a tabby cat next to Jax.

Jax watched as she applied a tiny clear patch to Sage's temple. He smiled. "Your planet is more evolved than I had previously thought," he murmured. A few moments later, he touched Sage's brow again and nodded. "A little better. But he needs true healing. It's like somebody tore a ragged hole inside his mind and he needs it closed. And if you have such things as psychic healers, I would dare say you summon them."

Rising, he turned. That was when he realized just how intently he was being studied. With a slow smile, he bared his fangs, focusing on Anni. "I can control my hunger, little sister," he murmured softly. "But I starve, and I ache. I shall return."

With that, he was gone, quicker than any of them could even track his movements.

Chapter Seven

Caris was coming out of her room, her hair braided back away from her face, light makeup applied, her lips slicked wine-red, gold dangles hanging from her ears, a smug little smile curving her face. It faded as she glimpsed Dustin slowly and painfully making his way inside. She saw his bloody, battered face and stopped, staring at him, her mouth open. "What in the hell happened to you?" she asked, her eyes wide and round.

He stared at her, flushing a dull red, with humiliation from what he had said, and from being pounded so easily into the dirt. "Your boyfriend took offense to something I said," he finally spat out through his swollen mouth.

Caris narrowed her eyes. Then she caught sight of Sage. "Sage..."

She was at his side before she even realized she had moved. "What happened, Morgan?" she demanded, running her hands over his torso, cupping his pale, graying face. "He was doing better this morning. He was fine. Did something—" Her eyes unfocused and she probed. "Damn it, why does he feel likes he's been drained..." her voice trailed off as she felt eyes on her.

Those eyes moved to Dustin.

"You." She rose slowly. "Exactly what did you say that Jax took offense to? And what does Sage have to do with it? Or do I need to ask?" she asked, her face flushing with anger.

"No," he said gruffly. "I don't guess you do." He slid his eyes to Sage, who lay still as death. Drained, Caris had said. Dustin was not a teleporter, and other than his unbelievable strength and size, he had no true power. But he knew what drained was. He could have done Sage serious harm. And Sage had saved them all yesterday.

The bad thing was, it wasn't the first time. Sage was a fucking hero, and that really burned his ass. Sage had saved him, had saved all of them, more than once and now because Dustin couldn't swallow hearing what had gone on behind closed doors, knowing he wasn't ever going to touch that smooth golden skin, or feel her soft, warm body—FUCK!

Slowly, stiffly, he turned and faced Morgan. "Do I need to go?"

Morgan shifted in his chair, hooking one ankle over his knee, steepling his long, graceful hands together in front of his face. His white hair was loose today, falling over his lean shoulders and chest in silky straight tresses. Those disconcerting ice blue eyes met Dustin's and Morgan lifted one shoulder in a casual shrug that did little to convince him that his leader wasn't seething with rage.

"That is up to you, Dustin," he said softly. "I would think you owe three people a very public apology, first of all, Caris.

"But beyond that…you will let this go. Completely and totally. She is out of your life. You will work together, when and if I say so. But beyond that, she does not exist for you. If you can't deal with that—hit the fucking road," Morgan said silkily. "If this happens again, you had better pray the vampire deals with you before I get my hands on you."

Quirking a silver-white brow at him, Morgan asked, "Do you need to ask what I'd do if I had my hands on you?"

Dustin's eyes revealed the answer and Morgan smiled coolly. "Her life, her choices are just that. Hers. And the next time I hear or see something like what has happened here, Dustin, you will be sorry. I will see to that. And you do not really want me angry, do you, Dustin? I don't know if I can control my temper as admirably as her vampire can."

Morosely, Dustin thought of his aching kidney, and of the fact that he'd be pissing blood for a week. Already sorry. Then he looked at Caris and sighed. The anger in Morgan's eyes was nothing compared to what he saw there.

Morgan's temper was a frightening thing, something nobody ever wanted to see loosed.

But right now, he was wondering if it wouldn't be better to face the silver-haired man, rather than the golden woman in front of him.

* * * * *

As far as bloodletting went, it was a satisfying kill. His belly was full. His cock ached, but he'd drive it into Caris that night and...Jax grinned as he ran back down the trail to her home.

The wild game here was scarce.

That would be a problem.

At least her home was surrounded by forest, that was some help. Life abounded in the distant mountains, so vibrant and rich he could taste it from here. He could hunt there if he must.

His fangs had retracted into their sheaths finally, and the bothersome ache in his jaws had faded away. The wind blew through his hair, caressed the skin of his face, neck and hands. There was nothing like the feel of life that ran through the body after a feeding.

Unless it was the fucking that followed.

He grinned.

Too bad there were so many people in Caris' house.

He came to a soundless stop outside her house and cocked his head, listening. A slow smile spread across his face. The mountain was slowly and scathingly being torn down into small, tiny little rocks, ground into pebbles beneath the sole of Caris' delicate little foot.

He padded on silent feet around the house, following the voices. They were in the room she called the library, filled with old…books? Yes, books and a machine she called a computer. It was like the nav-screen he used for reading, gaming, and entertainment back home.

"You arrogant, old-fashioned, mother-fucking son of a bitching jealous prick! What right do you have to tell me what I can and can't do? And what right do you have to question who I take to my bed?" she snarled. She stood no taller than Dustin's breastbone, but she hissed angrily into his face, and hammered his wide chest with her fist. "If I want to fuck every male I see, wherever I see him, it doesn't concern you, Dustin."

Dustin, wisely, was silent. His lips, nose and eyes were bruised and swollen.

"Damn your ass to hell and back, Dustin. If you didn't like it, you could have gone outside. What in the hell were you doing up, anyway? You've got a bloody suite. It's stocked, damn it. You could live happily in those rooms for a month and you came roaming out in the middle of the night and got offended when you heard me getting fucked! What were you expecting?

"This is my damn house and I can do what I want in it!" she shouted when he made no response.

Dustin blinked, and looked away. His face was red, underneath the colorful bruises.

"What in the flying fuck were you thinking? You saw what kind of shape Sage was in yesterday. Were you trying to kill him?" she shouted when he didn't reply.

"He was feeling good enough to get fucked, wasn't he?" Dustin muttered.

She punched him.

Through the window, Jax watched and grinned widely as her powerful little uppercut sent Dustin's head snapping back. She wasn't strong enough to knock him off his feet, but she sure as hell hurt him. "Bastard," she seethed. "Why don't you get it? I don't want you."

He smiled, then, a sad, odd little smile. He glanced out the window and met Jax's eyes. Jax lifted one brow. He had sensed him. How odd.

"You don't get it, Caris. I do understand—you don't want me, you never have and never will. But I still want you. And I'm always going to." He moved away, slowly, stiffly, but not showing any sign of the pain Jax knew he was feeling. Even through the glass and the distance, he could smell a strong scent of internal bleeding. Oh, he'd be all right, Jax had not done any severe damage.

But he was in some bad pain.

"I was wrong," Dustin said quietly. "I knew that then. I know it now. Sage was my friend—I may well have lost that. But nothing is going to change what I feel, Caris." He paused long enough to add, "We have troubles coming. I know it. If Morgan did not need me here, I'd get the hell out. He's gonna find a way to see it happen soon anyway.

"If I thought y'all might not need me, then I'd go. But I can't just walk away from what's coming, Caris. You couldn't either."

* * * * *

Caris was sitting in her chair, glaring into the distance when Jax came into the room. "Stupid fuck," she whispered, her eyes stinging with tears. "I've known him since I was a kid. He's always been—"

"In love with you?" he finished for her as he lifted her out of the chair and sat down, taking her onto his lap.

She flushed red. "You beat the hell out of him. I don't want it worse," she said flatly.

"He is lucky I did not give him worse."

"I meant I don't want you adding to it. If I'd been awake and seen him fighting Sage, I'd have probably strangled him," she snapped, her small hands clenching into tight fists. "Damn it, Sage could have died yesterday. It has happened, you know, when one of us has pushed too hard. I was a damn fool for letting what happened last night happen—"

"Sage was well enough. Otherwise he would not have woken up. His body wouldn't have let him," Jax interrupted, stroking a hand down her back, easing the tense muscles. He pulled the band from the end of her braid, freeing her hair from the thick, complicated cable and stroking it until it hung free and loose around her shoulders. "Do not feel guilty. You had nothing to do with why he is lying in the state he is in."

She flushed, her pretty golden eyes flashing with fire. "I knew Dustin was in the house. If I had stopped to think—but damn it, I shouldn't have to!"

"No. You should not. And you will not," Jax said easily. As he spoke, he slid one hand between her thighs and pressed.

Her eyes went wide and rounded. "Oh," she whispered. He shifted again, spreading her legs and pulling them so that she was straddling him, then he rocked his cock against her cleft.

"I've a need to be inside you," he said roughly. "I went too long without feeding and hunted an animal. But I need sex and I need it now. I thought I could wait until tonight, but looking at you, smelling you..." He pushed his cock upward against her cleft and rocked, shuddering as the scent of her arousal filled the air. "I need you."

She lifted her hands to her shirt and he brushed them away, reaching for the buttons and jerking it open. He shredded the heavy, sturdy material of her jeans and opened the tab of his flight pants before tumbling them out of the chair and onto the floor. He pushed her to her hands and knees, her round little ass in the air, and mounted her roughly, driving into her hard and fast, growling as her tight little pussy closed over his cock wet and eager, like a fist.

She yelped and squirmed against his abrupt invasion, then moaned when Jax reached around and pinched her clit. Her golden-brown hair slithered and fell around her shoulders, spilling to the floor as he rode her harder, his heavy weight taking her down until her torso collapsed onto the floor. Only his big hands kept her ass and hips in the air while he pulled his cock out and drove back in, growling out roughly with pleasure as her slick, wet tissues hugged him snugly.

He pulled out, his thick cock gleaming wetly from her cream and then he surged slowly back inside, smiling as she moaned.

Caris shuddered when she felt his fingers probing her ass. "I cannot wait," he whispered hotly. "So tiny, so snug." He slicked some of her cream around the pink pucker and pushed his finger in, listening to the ragged moan she tried to muffle. He slowed the pumping of his hips and started to plunge his finger in and out, wiggling it a little, stretching the narrow passage.

She keened softly and tried to pull away but he gripped her hip and growled roughly in warning. "Be still, Caris. You will like this," he promised darkly as he added a second finger.

She stiffened. The burning pain increased as he started to pump his long, thick fingers inside her ass. Like it, hell. And there was no way—oh, shit. Jax reached around with his other hand and flicked her clit, stroking it busily. His cock slid from her body and he shifted so that she was between his thighs, giving him access to her clit and her ass.

A violent shudder racked her body as he drove his finger inside her just as he started to stimulate her clit. Leaning over her, he caught her mouth in a deep kiss, driving his tongue inside, nipping her lip, teasing her into kissing him back as he penetrated her anus ever deeper.

Yes, you will like it, he purred into her mind as her hips started to rock against the maddening caress of his fingers. He sucked her tongue into his mouth and bit down roughly before tearing his mouth from her and kissing his way down her throat.

Like it? Damnation, I won't survive it... Her skin felt too tight, too small, for the hot, burgeoning needs that flooded her, intense and overpowering. A fine sweat broke out on her body as he brought her right to the edge of orgasm with his artful play on her clit. Then he stopped, urged her lower, and started to fuck her ass roughly with his fingers. Caris started to scream, her body shaking, hot and tight.

Jax felt his fangs drop as he watched his fingers drive back inside the tight, silken well of her ass. She rocked back helplessly, driving the sweet curve of her butt back against his hand while she moaned and squirmed and whimpered. With his free hand, he brought her up, shoved her hair aside, arched her neck and struck just as she came. Her anal sheath locked around his fingers, her supple, slim body pressed up and back against him while she screamed and whimpered and sobbed.

He took only a little—just desperate for her taste. Then he pushed her onto her back while she was still climaxing and mounted her roughly, driving his cock deep inside her convulsing pussy while he caught her hands and pinned them high over her head.

He kissed her blindly, smearing her mouth with her own blood as he jackhammered his cock into her, harder and harder. She arched underneath him, tightening again, and Jax tore his mouth from hers to rasp, "Again...come again, Caris."

Pulling out, he drove back into the sweet, wet heat of her pussy, harder and harder as he growled against her neck a second time, "Come, Caris...come for me."

Her eyes had gone blank and she was already there, the minute spasms in her sheath growing ever tighter until she was locked down around him like a wet, living vise. He pounded into her, growling out her name, loving her silken tissues hugging his cock. Loving the hot feel of her blood warm in his belly, the scent of her sex in the air.

The ever strengthening caress of her orgasm tightened around his cock until he could no longer hold his own back. He burrowed deep inside her, the head of his cock lodged at the mouth of her womb, Caris sobbing out his name as he started to come, flooding her womb with hot, wet jets of sperm. His cock jerked and throbbed inside her, pumping the last of his seed deep as her lashes fluttered down and moments later, she went limp under his hands. Jax pushed harder into her, groaning, and holding still while he rode his orgasm to the end.

Then he withdrew and rolled to his side, pulling her against him.

This was going to be a problem.

He couldn't very well go into frenzy every damn time he fucked her. Her mortal body could not take it. And he had just proven that he lost control even after he had fed.

Ah, it was a problem...

* * * * *

And he was currently staring at another one.

The body was that of someone young and innocent and pure, but the eyes were evil. Jax withdrew his hand from the invader's forehead and rose, smirking at him as the thing lashed out and tried to ensnare him.

He deflected the clumsy swipe, the uncontrolled power and said, "I told you — I am not such easy prey."

The boy/man sat there, watching them, his gaze ripe with the foul anger that ate at him.

He beckoned silently to Caris and led her outside, leaving a sullen Dustin to watch over the invader while they spoke.

"We have to have the other body, the one this soul belongs to," Jax murmured to Caris. He watched through the window, keeping his voice low. "The body can't survive without the soul, Caris. It can't. They found a way to switch them. We will switch them back, but to do that, we need the other body. It must be holding the boy."

"Any ideas?" Morgan asked wryly, joining them with a speaking glance cast toward where the boy/man waited and watched.

Jax turned and watched as Morgan drifted around the corner. The man's long white hair was flowing freely today, blowing around his face in the breeze. His pale blue eyes were blank and cool, but Jax could smell the rage that all but bubbled under his skin. Too much had happened in the past few days and none of it was good.

"A bit of one, perhaps," Jax said cautiously. "But I understand your gifts too little. And I do not know if any of you have what I seek."

"Well…why don't you tell us?" Morgan asked sardonically, cocking a brow and waiting.

Caris studied him with narrowed eyes and before Jax could stop her, she reached up and touched his cheek. His eyes met hers as the knowledge poured from him into her, and she said quietly to Morgan, "He wants a teleporter. Jax thinks he can follow the man's trail to the boy and hold him that way and have the teleporter go in and get him."

Arching a brow, Jax asked softly, "Will it work?"

"You would need one who was a strong enough psychic to link with you," she said, troubled. "Sage's psychic powers are chaotic at times. Unless he's bonded with the one he is communicating with, it might not work. His other gifts are more reliable." She slid Morgan a look. "Do we have a teleporter who can go in and out with a traveler? Somebody other than Sage, who has the psychic skills?"

"That would be me," a low husky voice said.

Morgan stiffened. "Ari, didn't I warn you about teleporting?" he asked coolly, even though his blue eyes were flashing with something Caris rarely saw—nerves and aggravation. He kept his back to the newly arrived agent as he stared into the distance, not turning to greet Ari.

Her full red lips curved in a sardonic smile before she slid her dark gold gaze to Caris and a real smile spread. "Hey, kid. You look wonderful," she said quietly. Her eyes, spiked with long, thick lashes, moved on to Jax and they lit with interest. "Hmmm. And I wonder why...who might you be?"

Jax arched a brow at the hand the woman was holding out to him and slowly reached out to take it, aware of the deft, subtle probe she attempted. He deflected it, of course, as he answered softly, "A friend of Caris'."

"Such an interesting one," Ari mused, waggling her brows at Caris.

Then she looked back at Morgan who had finally deigned to glance her way. "Oh, sire, I must beg your forgiveness," she mocked lightly. "The others are in town. I wanted to make sure this place wasn't a crater before we drove out here—didn't want to lead them into a trap. Too many are young recruits. Believe it or not, big guy, I do have a brain."

"What exactly do you need somebody like me for?" she asked, cocking her head and studying them.

Caris sighed and said, "Come inside and I'll show you."

Ari studied the house, following them down to the old bomb shelter with a wrinkle of her nose. "I hate underground places like this."

Her eyes landed on the boy as Caris pushed the door open and gestured her inside.

A soft smile had been forming but it faded immediately.

Jax's opinion solidified. This woman was a good one. She hissed like a cat and drew back three steps, simply looking at the creature in front of her. "What in the hell is going on?" she rasped, her normally husky voice an urgent whisper. "That is no child."

"No. It is not," Jax agreed. "However, I believe I can find the child who belongs in that body. With some help."

"Ergo, the teleporter with psychic skill who can take a traveler," she said quietly, moving a little closer. "How did they do this?"

"I don't know, Ari," Caris said softly. "But we have to find out." Her golden hair framed her face, tumbling into her troubled eyes. "If they can do this sort of thing, we have to wonder what else they can do."

Jax said softly, "Not wonder. We must know. Else, you are in danger."

"I can't zip around at random the way Sage does. I can go in and get the body holding the child and come back here, easily enough. I can't do it a dozen times the way Sage does, but I can do it. My stronger skill, as you and Morgan know, is telepathy." She slid Jax a look and asked, "Exactly what sort of help do you need?"

"A focus, of sorts. To be true, I am not totally certain I can do this, but I must try," he said slowly, meeting her golden gaze. Her spiked black hair, red-slicked lips, the large gold hoops, everything about her made Caris think of a gypsy, and if it wasn't for the fact that she and Ari were friends of a sort, she'd be a bit worried.

But then Jax moved and aligned himself at her back, brushing his lips across her neck, resting one hand on her hip. Ari grinned at them, shaking her head. "So when do we get started?"

"It might help," Morgan suggested wryly, "if Jax knew exactly what you could do."

"First things first. Let's round up the rest of the crew," Ari said. "Anybody up for a trip into town?"

"I'd like some…other clothing," Jax said, glancing down at his flight suit. The self cleaning mechanism had kept it in good shape, but still…he eyed the jeans Morgan wore. Those looked more comfortable anyway. "Caris?" He added silently, *Perhaps we could find a thing or two…*

She blushed as he sent her images of his homeworld, sex toys designed to help prepare a woman to accept a man anally, images of Jax forcing a thick gleaming toy slowly into her bottom. Her breath shuddered out of her and she closed her fingers tightly around his forearm, her nails biting lightly even through the heavy material. *Hmmm, so they do have such things?* he teased.

Chapter Eight

Jax eyed the cockpit of the small craft with distaste. It was about four meters long, had eight seats, cylindrical, and the wheels were even now retreating into the base as it started to rise into the air. "What is the purpose of this?" he asked as Dustin settled at the controls.

The mountain didn't answer. Caris replied, "It's an ALTV, Air/Land Transport Vehicle. We can do quick, short air transport, but also use it for city driving as well." She used a mental picture link to "describe" driving as Dustin shot up quickly and punched it, sending them screaming into the searing blue sky.

Caris folded her hand around Jax's and said through gritted teeth, "Dustin isn't going to make this a pleasant trip. He's a demon on the tracks. And he's still sulking."

"The tracks?"

"Hmmm. He's a space jock in his spare time. Races sky cars," she answered, sending more images, tiny little silver bullets, winging through sky courses dodging other racers.

"He's the best. And he's certifiably insane."

Des Moines loomed on the horizon before any of them lost their lunches, but with the exception of Dustin, and Jax, all five of them climbed out shaky and pale. *If you don't like his driving tactics, why ride with him?* Jax asked, supporting her with a nonchalant arm under her elbow.

Habit. We've had a few close calls, and Dusty can lose anybody.

Ari, Miguel and Morgan slid Dustin irritated looks, but he just smiled blandly at them as he paid for the holding fee at the docking station. Morgan flicked a glance at his watch. "I know we all have some business to attend to, and we can't just gather up our...friends and head out so quickly. So let's split up," he said quietly, moving in and speaking softly right against Caris' ear. "Three hours. Then we meet where Ari and I discussed. Ari and Miguel are together, Dustin and I will stay together. You and Jax will stay together. I doubt I have to spell this out, but no splitting up. Period. We're being picked off one by one and it ends now."

Caris smiled and turned her face, brushing her lips against Morgan's smooth cheek in a soft kiss as she whispered, "No spelling out needed. I'm no fool. And I understand." Then she took Jax's hand and guided him off the landing dock and down the moving glide, not once glancing back. She responded to Ari's sassy, "Don't do anything I wouldn't do," with a sly "And exactly what wouldn't you do?"

* * * * *

Ari narrowed her eyes as Morgan informed her just who her "buddy" was. Not that she had anything against Miguel. He was sexy as sin, sweet as chocolate. But she had her eyes focused on Morgan.

And the silver-haired bastard knew it. As Dustin and Morgan exited the landing bay, she sighed and met Miguel's eyes. "Don't sweat it, babe," he told her, winking. "He's no more happy 'bout this than you. But he can't be taking his eyes off Dusty right now. The big man is an accident waiting to happen."

Sliding her green eyes to the Puerto Rican agent, she arched a black brow and asked, "Really? Exactly what have I been missing?"

He hooked a friendly arm around her neck and guided her out of the landing bay. "Oh, but have I got stories and stories and stories to be telling you. Let's see to our errands, as Morgan has called them, and then we'll find us a bar, and I will tell all."

* * * * *

From across the street, Morgan stood in the doorway as Dustin signed in at a standing free clinic to have his ribs and nose checked. He watched with thinly veiled rage as Miguel and Ari walked away from the parking station. Ari Rayborne—what had he done to bring her back into his life?

And why in hell was he so fucking pissed about seeing her walking arm in arm with one of his agents? Shit, if Miguel was stupid enough to hook up with the likes of Ari, the fool deserved to have his heart ripped out, his cock sucked dry, and a hole the size of Kansas left in his soul.

* * * * *

Caris slowed to a reluctant stop outside the store. Jax had his hand wrapped firmly around the thick cable of her braid, so really what choice did she have? He had bypassed quite a few stores, the seamier ones, so for that she was thankful, but damn it, she hadn't ever done any actual shopping in a store like this.

She'd always bought her toys online and now he was taking her inside?

"What about money? I mean, you don't have any yet, and I..."

He slid her a look from his dark blue eyes and she swallowed. "Okay. I mean, yeah, I can buy—"

"I have money," he said softly. "Miguel was quite...impressed by something I had. A stone he thought would be worth a...pretty penny, he said. It was—" he made a circle with his thumb and forefinger, two inches across, "and dark blue. I have several more back at the house. He paid me, ah, two thousand? Yes, two thousand and five hundred in cold hard American standard." He mimicked Miguel's slightly Hispanic accent perfectly.

Caris' eyes narrowed. *And he probably ripped you off, the American way,* she mused. "I want to see these stones," she said, forgetting some of her discomfort. But the minute she went back to studying the plain wooden door, she remembered it all. The Den was one of the more popular adult stores in the United Federal States of America and catered to a little classier set than the average adult store did, which is why they had ended up catching a ride on one of the skycabs to get here.

Jax led her through the doors while she was still pondering Miguel and she turned bright red the minute she stepped inside. Jax chuckled and led her deeper into the room, casting the approaching woman a dismissing glance. She smiled, inclined her head, and retreated to the desk without a word.

"Hmmm, this will work well, I am thinking," he murmured, studying what he saw before him. "This will most definitely suit my purposes." He guided Caris in front of him and leaned down to whisper in her ear, "You've toys of your own, yes?" Splaying his hand against her belly, he rocked his hips and stroked his cock against her ass. "Something for your sweet, tight little ass, we need. What else?"

Her face flushed and her breathing kicked up as she shook her head.

"If you'll not tell me, then the choosing is up to me," he warned her teasingly.

Oh, hell…

She opened her mouth, but the spit had all dried up and she couldn't speak anyway. She watched in terrified, aroused fascination as he reached up and selected a wide, tapered butt plug, a silver bullet, an expandable vibrating butt plug, a telescoping vibrator, restraints… "Umm, exactly how much are you planning to get?"

He laughed. "Exactly how much are you willing to let me?" he replied as he added lubricant to his selection, and pretended to search for more.

Caris whimpered as he lowered his head and whispered, "I am anxious for tonight, Caris. Very, very anxious."

They followed with a quick trip to a clothing store and had just finished when it was time to head to the address Ari had given her. It was in a low-class area, but not so low-class that the cops regularly cased it. Ari had made a wise choice. She could recognize some of the emotion ranges coming from it as she slid from the cab, holding the lone bag Jax had let her carry. Of course, it was the plain black bag from The Den. She couldn't touch it without hyperventilating.

Damn it…tonight.

She felt Ari as the other woman moved up behind her. "How many more roommates am I taking home tonight? I can sense five," she said as she folded her hand over Jax's.

"Nine," Ari said with a sigh. "I didn't want to bring any more." Miguel stood at her shoulder, his normally laughing eyes serious and somber. "If we have too many at one location, we're just asking for trouble. The rest...well, Morgan's gonna get pissed at my presumption, but I picked out some 'lieutenants' and told them to round up whoever they could and find a safe house. We'll be hearing from them as soon as they are settled.

"We need to get organized. We can't keep doing this 'fly-by-night' deal," Ari finished, shaking her head. "Morgan has got to know that by now."

"How many are there?" Jax inquired.

"Firewalkers, or agents?" Caris asked. "There's no telling how many Firewalkers. Not all of them fight with us. Many of them live their entire lives pretending to be normal, not one of us. We have more than two hundred agents, but Ari's right. We have no true organization. Morgan's running the show, and he's doing the best he can, but none of us have any real training in anything that could be called good solid, well, technique. We would have been discovered if we'd tried to go through the militia or into Police or Security." She gave a frustrated groan. "We can't keep this up."

"I can help," Jax whispered softly, wrapping one brawny arm around her waist. "Let me talk to Morgan. I can help."

They moved inside and found Morgan and Dustin were already there. Caris found the few she recognized, and two faces she didn't know at all. Besides the two she didn't know, one young teleporter, and a healer she was familiar with, thank God. There was another healer, two empaths, a pyro, and a telekinetic. And a partridge in a pear tree, she told herself wryly.

The healers were more than welcome.

The teleporter could be a problem. He was already looking edgy.

The pyro was looking at Morgan with something akin to worship in her big gray eyes. Behind that, she had the anger and attitude of a young adult who had been forced into far too much.

Then all eyes focused on Jax and widened.

Caris stifled a snicker and moved forward to make introductions, keeping it short and sweet, leaving out the part about *He's my lover and he likes to bite me and drink my blood while we're fucking. And we've already had a ménage with Sage. Sounds like fun, huh?*

Somehow, she didn't think it would make any of them look at him with any less apprehension.

Chapter Nine

The two ALTV's landed in front of Caris' houses several hours later. Dustin took them through a number of evasive maneuvers, after going over each machine with a fine-tooth comb, making certain no tag devices had been planted.

Caris, Jax and Ari left their shields wide open, making sure they could sense if anyone was on their back trail.

When they were as sure as they could be nobody was following them, they let Dustin know it was okay to land.

They disappeared into the house as Morgan and Dustin took the ALTVs deep into the mountains after loading a jetbike into the cargo bay. Just in case... "A fucking waste of a fine transport," Miguel muttered, shaking his head as they zipped off toward the horizon.

Ari shrugged her shoulders. "This is Morgan, for crying out loud. The man is loaded. He'll just buy more."

She turned and looked at her charges, most of them frightfully young. The pyro was pouting because she hadn't been invited to go along. "Get over it, Jeza. I think Morgan and Dusty can handle this on their own. They don't need a tagalong to worry about."

"I can handle myself," the tall mixed-race girl said, her gray eyes flashing fire. A red gleam started to glow behind those misty gray eyes, a sure sign of anger in a pyrokinetic.

"Yes, I'm sure you can," Ari said sweetly. "That's why I had to haul your bony ass out of lockup, right? Those federal marshals weren't really getting ready to put you into a psyn-iron box and fry you, were they?"

Jeza's eyes narrowed and she hissed, advancing on the shorter woman. Caris slid between them and met Jeza's eyes. "Step down, kid. You are new, so I guess maybe you just don't know the rules. We'll take that into consideration. Rookies don't go on missions for a good three years. They train, they study, they learn control. Which you are obviously lacking—" she dropped her eyes to the red glow hovering around Jeza's hands. "I can make sure it's a hell of a lot longer for you if you don't cool down, and I mean fast. Is that what you want?"

"Who the fuck are you?"

Caris arched a golden brow and said, "Your hostess. So unless you want to go out on your...bony ass, where the feds can easily find you and finish the job...?"

"I don't like threats," Jeza said in a low, rasping growl. The glow around her hands had started to throb and it was now a fire, albeit a small one, but a fire.

Caris cocked a brow at her, lashing down the tiny fear in the pit of her belly. She knew how to handle a pyro, and she wasn't without her own defenses, but damn it, why did pyros always have such easily lit fuses?

"This isn't a threat. It's a statement of fact. You're behaving like a child, so I'll treat you like one. You want to be one of us? Ride along with your hero Morgan? He won't take you across the driveway with this kind of temper, much less someplace where it matters. I've known him for years—he doesn't even know your name," Caris said coolly, dismissively. "He'll never care to know it with you acting like this. Temperamental children are of no interest to him."

Jeza's eyes widened with surprised hurt, jealousy, and the fire started to flicker and eat more of the space surrounding her. "I don't like bitches like you."

"Tsk," Caris said. "I can't tell you how much that hurts."

"Me, I don' like spoiled li'l brats," Miguel drawled from where he had flopped when they had retreated into the house.

Jax was reclining against the wall, still watching through lowered lashes, debating whether or not to intervene. He could scent her nervousness, but Caris wasn't really concerned, just a bit edgy. However, the girl — she was a wild thing. He did not like that.

The power inside her flared and her eyes gleamed red. Pushing off the wall...but too late. Miguel had flung something around Jeza.

And the lady wasn't happy.

Miguel rose from the couch and ambled over to study his barrier which was a small cylinder, only large enough to hold Jeza. If she moved or shifted, she was going to touch it. If her fire spilled out, it was going to burn one person...her. "It was jus' some friendly advice, *amiga*, and you shouldn't take offense to friendly advice," he said, smiling amicably. "Now you be good and still, and when Morgan gets back, we can all talk friendly like. When you understand the law of the land, and are willing to play nice —"

"Lemme out of here now!" she shrieked, her long golden braids falling into her face as she started to shudder and vibrate with fury.

Miguel clucked his tongue. "No can do, *amiga*. You've already shown us just how hot your blood runs. Can't have you hurting anybody, now can we?" he asked, winking at her. He smiled easily at Caris who was shaking her head and muttering, "Why me?"

Ari was laughing against her will. "Honey, if I had known you were gonna be this much trouble from the get-go, I just might have left you in that psyn-iron box," she drawled to Jeza. She glanced at Miguel and asked, "Can you move her out of the doorway?"

When Jeza was lifted up like a bag of laundry by an invisible force, she shrieked and hissed at the indignity of it, then subsided into sullen fury, glaring at Miguel. He smiled his megawatt smile at her and whispered teasingly, "Maybe if you act nice, I'll let you out. We can go upstairs...I don't mind getting singed...no? Ah, well. It was worth a try."

* * * * *

Ari and Jax sat facing each other, the not-boy in a body-sized shielding of Miguel's making. Jax spared a brief moment to give Ari a sympathetic smile as the evil eyes in that innocent face ran over her body as she had lowered herself to the floor. Jax had linked his mind with the intruder's, blocking the curly blond hair, the charming smile, the look of innocence. Instead he focused on the foul, crawling stench of perversion, discontent, and evil as he waded through the mire of the man's mind.

Corruption, the need to control the power of the freakish, even though he was one of them. Far, far away, Jax followed that train of thought, even as the man started to understand and fight him. From without, Caris wrapped her own bonds around the intruder and silenced him, keeping him from alerting anybody — a gift Jax didn't realize she had.

Ari smiled. "Caris is full of surprises, Jax," she murmured as she accepted the hand Jax offered. "But she's gonna find out one day, she has her limits. She's pushed them too far already. Or let others push her to them."

Jax's eyes flickered as a static shock ran through him at Ari's touch, while she absorbed the link through his mind. Now that was she focusing on him, he could see more. The room.

They had locked the little boy in a room that was hardly the size of a closet. Oh, he was being cleaned and cared for, because the body belonged to that of a compatriot. But they were torturing the child inside, keeping him in the dark, keeping him afraid. Keeping him lost.

"Hush, cher. I'm taking you outta that place, right now," Ari murmured. The world just fell away from her as she followed the link, forgetting Jax's words of caution as she absorbed the feelings from that boy. She needed to put the boy inside his own body, and the man inside of his, so they could punish him. Right and proper, as her mama would have said.

Right and proper.

She found him huddling in the dark, rocking against the wall, wearing nothing more than a T-shirt and underwear. A big strong male body, cuddled into a tiny fetal ball, whimpering and crying, "Take me back to Mama, please," his voice was hoarse from days of crying.

What had they done to his mama? she wondered.

Unless Morgan knew, the poor boy would probably never see her again. Ari moved over him, squinting to see inside the dark, hurrying as voices in the hall grew louder. "Hey. C'mon, let's get outta this dark old place."

"Who's there?" he asked, whimpering, turning his tear-stained face her way.

"A friend, *mon ami*. Somebody who wants to help, *cher*. C'mon, before the nasty boys come back in here and try to scare you some more."

"They won't tell me where my mom is. Will you?" he asked, lifting his chin in defiance.

"Ah, *bebè*, if I knew, I'd tell you. But I don't. Nothing good will happen if you stay here. And that is a fact. You wanna stay here all alone in the dark, in a body that isn't yours?"

He looked down at the hands, so much bigger than his own. She could see his lip quivering in the dimness of the room. "No. I don't like this. He feels…dirty. And at least you didn't lie to me." The sigh that came from that childish mind was far too world-weary. Ari wanted to cry with him as he stood and reached out, like the child he truly was, and waited for her to take his hand.

Wrapping him in her arms, Ari felt the world fall away just as the door to the room flew open and voices started rising, the low boom of a sonic weapon firing.

She never even noticed the burning in her arm until they had already settled down in Caris' living room and the boy saw his body there. And he started to scream.

Ignoring the laser-induced cut on her arm, Ari moved to the boy with Caris, shushing him as she wrapped her arms around him. "It's all right, *bèbe*. It's all right."

It was the next morning that Caris found the boy sleeping outside the locked door to the cell where the intruder was kept. It was startling to see the boy staring out at her from the man's eyes. But a boy he was, never mind that the body was that of a middle-aged man.

His name was Erik.

Just Erik.

He couldn't remember his last name. Nor his mama's name, or where they had lived, or how long ago he had been taken away from her. Just that he could make things float with his eyes, he thought. Or he had used to be able to.

They had done something when they had made this bizarre body switch.

Or soul switch.

That was what it was, Caris was thinking as Miguel came ambling through the door, running a hand through his hair, and glancing at her then at the man curled in a ball and sucking his thumb. "Ya gotta admit, that's an odd sight, *amiga*," he mused, shaking his head. "And the boss man is confused as hell about how to fix this one."

Caris wasn't so certain that fixing it would be that hard. They really needed to know how it had been done in the first place, but she couldn't help but notice, even as the boy slept, he kept inching closer to the door, or trying to.

They weren't in their natural state.

And they wanted to be. Reaching out, she lay one hand on his cheek, and her other on his chest. Unrest, unease, even more than there had been last night. Edgy, awkward...yes.

"Miguel, you want to help me try something really stupid?" she asked, flashing Miguel a quick glance.

Miguel's eyes flicked to her warily. "I don't like the sound of that, *chica*. Me, I do stupid things. You don't."

"Well, this might not be too stupid. But I need a safety. You are my safety...just in case. I think they wanna be back where they belong," she said. "But the man will try to hurt the boy," she said quietly. "I think I can fix it. But I don't want that boy being hurt. I don't want him left unprotected."

"You want me to keep them close but apart, right?" Miguel asked, one thick black brow winging up as he followed the path of her thoughts with amazing accuracy.

"I can't do this with a shield up. They can't be apart. But once it happens, you have to shield that man, that sick, soulless bastard," Caris said, sliding her eyes to the door, where behind it, the man was waiting inside the boy's body. "I think once they are together, their bodies are going to let it happen naturally. That man wants the boy dead-- I don't know if he knows anything or not, but the man is evil and we can't risk him hurting the kid."

"I'm here for ya, *chica*," Miguel smiled solemnly, looping an arm around her neck and studying the boy/man lying on the floor. "Ready now?"

"No time like the present." And if they did it now, while Jax was out hunting and the others were scattered throughout the house, they were less likely to get caught until after they had already started.

Caris settled down in the basement across from Erik and his borrowed body with a gentle, reassuring smile on her face as Miguel keyed the laz-lock on the shelter open. When the intruder spat out, "Get away from me, you filthy diseased fuck-freak," Miguel just laughed and flicked a hand toward him. "That's a funny one, *amigo*. Now be nice. Don't make me remember I don' like you. And before I decide to wrap that mouth shut. I have company for you."

The greed and want in those blue eyes was instantaneous. Caris flicked her gaze to Miguel and he flashed her a cocky grin. "Already done, babe. You lemme know when you are ready," he murmured, sliding his hands into his pockets and propping his shoulder against a smooth black beam.

The man/boy ignored them as he leaped forward, a hungry, animalistic growl in his throat, only to smack head first into an invisible barrier. Behind it, Erik, in the body they had forced on him, scuttled back, whimpering. Caris slid her eyes questioningly to Miguel and he nodded. She crossed through with a smile and knelt by Erik. "Shhh, he won't hurt you. I'll make sure of it. I'm going to make sure he's good and still and quiet. We just want to get you back where you belong," Caris whispered, stroking her hand down his arm as his back came up against another black beam. "Will you trust me?"

Erik whimpered, cuddling his face against her arm. "I don't like him. He feels dirty."

"Then let's fix it," Caris whispered.

Erik nodded, his lip quivering.

Miguel strode forward, his lighthearted demeanor dying, his face switching to stone as he prepared to become the protector, leaving the smiling teasing joker behind. His eyes slid to the stolen body of the boy, pinning the evil creature inside as he purred, "You try to harm him, you will die. And I will enjoy it."

"Go fuck yourself," he hissed.

Miguel blinked, lowering his lashes slowly. Raising his fingers, he trailed them across the barrier, letting it dissolve as he stared into the intruder's eyes. Whispering,

"You remember my words, *cabron,* or you will know pain like you have never felt as you take your last breath."

Caris felt a shiver of fear run down her spine, even though the words weren't directed at her. So many forgot the danger that lurked below Miguel's laughing, teasing surface. Even the dark evil inside the boy's body stilled for the briefest moment before he turned his malevolent eyes on Caris and his true body, snarling, "You should never have tried this—they will make you pay, stupid fools."

Caris laughed throatily. "They were the fools, thinking they could do this and we would tolerate it. None harm our children and get away with it. We do not allow it."

Turning her eyes to the boy, she nodded gently and said, "Get up. It's time." She rested her hands in the middle of his back and stood behind him, a little to the side so she had a clear view of Miguel who was forcibly lifting the struggling intruder to his feet as he kicked and hissed, trying to sink his teeth into Miguel's hand. "Trying to fight a man while stuck in a child's body, not a good bargain on your end, *zurramato.*"

"I'll kill you when I'm in my body…" he panted. "Are you sure you want to switch me?" the man inside the boy's body growled, his voice growing eerily deeper as Miguel forced him closer and closer to his true body.

Miguel simply said, "I can't properly rip you apart until you are back where you belong." With that, he and Caris shoved them together and Miguel stared at Caris' face, waiting.

The door upstairs opened and voices flooded the stairwell as Caris waited, watching as the two bodies fell screaming to the floor, smoke pouring from the skin, the eyes, the mouth. Their eyes began to glow and each one latched hands onto the arms of the other. A shocked, pained gasp from the boy's mouth as the man sobbed, the cry of a poor, wounded boy as he screeched, "Mama!"

Then the boy's head whipped around and he was staring at Caris with the gleaming, glowing eyes of a Firewalker child. He shot up out of the scrambling grasp of the man's hands, the look of a panicked child on his face as he backed away.

The man was still staring around, rather blindly, his eyes glowing with a colorless, vague glow, like a streetlight through the fog as he swung his hand around blindly, snarling, "Come here, you little snotty brat. I'm going to rip your bloody heart out. Nothing but an animal anyway—"

"Oops," Miguel drawled as he moved forward and kicked the blind man's hands and knees out from under him, sending him sprawling on his face.

"Fucker!"

Caris cuddled Erik against her, one ear muffled against her shoulder, covering the other with her hand as the man tried to scramble to his feet, hissing and swearing in a hate-filled, hideous voice. "I'm gonna kill you, you disgusting, perverted freak. Smother that freak of a brat, then I'm gonna gag that pretty little bitch and show her what it's like to get fucked by a real man, not a fucking freak of nature—"

Miguel tsked under his breath, stepping outside the shield and turning around to study the man with mock sorrow just as Jax lunged down the stairs with murder in his eyes. "Sorry, my friend...I made that man a promise,"

Miguel murmured. "He wasn't gonna scare that kid again. And he just did."

Jax rammed face first into the faintly gleaming shield and swore as it singed him lightly. "Drop the shield, Miguel," Jax purred softly, stroking his hand over the air just above the shield, the crackling energy between him and the shield painting the air red.

"No, *amigo*." Miguel paced forward, cocking his head and studying the man inside the small bubble as the other Firewalkers from upstairs gathered around them.

"Miguel, drop the shield."

"He won't, Jax," Caris said as she rose, cradling the boy and studying his face, lowering her shields completely, as she so rarely did. Before Miguel did what couldn't be undone, she needed to make sure.

The guileless eyes of childhood, pure love, pure hope, pure innocence and joy, somewhat shadowed, but still there, shone back at her, out of an angelic, sweet face. Eyes bright with tears, bright with fear, he reached up and wrapped his arms around her neck, cuddling closer as he turned his face away from the man who had stolen his body for so long.

"Shall I show you the things I can do to those who defy me?" Jax growled, moving closer to Miguel, fangs dropped in anger.

Miguel's eyes were gleaming, shot through with bolts that resembled lightning as he moved to the barrier.

In a soft warning voice, Caris murmured, "You don't want to touch him right now, Jax. He's dangerous. This is one of his more unpleasant stages." She passed by him, stroking one hand down his arm before she headed for the stairs.

A rough growl slid from Jax's throat as he moved closer to Miguel, his dark blue eyes flashing with rage as he reached out, fingers extended for Miguel's throat. But miniature bolts of lightning leaped out at him as the space narrowed to inches, singing his skin, streaking down his arm, sending him to his knees. Swearing in pain, he cradled his arm to his chest.

"By the Suns!" Jax swore, falling back and staring up at Miguel who was focused on the shield, not even aware of Jax. The surface of the shield was now laced with streaks and dancing bolts of lightning. The orb started to shrink, closing in on the man within, who was now rising and staring with bleary, but seeing eyes at Miguel.

"Lemme out of this...this fucking cage," he rasped, curling his lip, tossing his head arrogantly.

"Shut up," Miguel said flatly, tossing his raven hair out of his eyes. His gaze narrowed and one black brow lifted as a different kind of shield formed, this one flat, over the man's mouth, keeping him silent as the shield continued to tighten around him.

The door swung shut behind Caris and Anni mewled in her throat, closing her eyes and turning away, taking to the stairs as the lightning dancing on the surface started to leap across the shield, flaying the man's skin, burning him.

Jax moved away, settling on his heels, watching as the lightning started to engulf the man, slowly, slowly. It was a slow, painful death, not a death by fire, or by blood loss, but slow, excruciating death by suffocation. The orb shrank down upon him, slowly smashing his lungs, crushing his chest.

Once his heart no longer beat, Miguel released the shield and let it fall. The corpse fell limply to the ground, crushed, blood oozing from a hundred tiny cuts.

With a small, solemn smile, he said, "You were warned." The lightning fire of death still danced in his eyes as he turned and stared at the other Firewalkers before crossing the room. They parted around him and let him go through, careful not to touch the flesh of his still deadly body.

It was later that night, hours after Morgan and Dustin had returned, hours after they had explained what she and Miguel had done, that she settled beside Sage on the couch, folding her legs up under her and propping her chin in her palm. He was pale still, face shadowed by a heavy growth of beard, his hazel eyes weary and shaded by pain.

"A healer is going to be taking a look at you," she said firmly.

Sage slid her a sideways look. "No," he said implacably. "I'm tired, and my head hurts. That is all. I don't need a healer."

Caris smiled sweetly and sidled a little closer. "Yes you do. And you're going to let her treat you," she whispered in his ear. "I will make it worth your while."

He snorted. "Don't tempt a dying man," he muttered, letting his aching head fall back to the cushions of the couch.

She rested her head on his shoulder, the familiarity soothing her. Sage had been there...for years. Since she had been a child. Morgan had found her parents, found her. And Sage had been with him since he had been a boy.

She and Sage had been friends since childhood. Connecting her mind to his was like coming home.

Truth or dare? she teased him in silent communication.

Too tired for games, darlin', he told her, turning his face to rub his cheek against her hair. *Besides, I don't want that pretty-boy savage of yours to come back here and kill me.*

She smiled against his shoulder. *He likes you. You're safe. Okay…don't wanna play, then I'll make it easy and give you the truth, real quick. And it's daring, so that makes it more fun. You understand fantasies, don't you, Sage?*

She felt his body tense with surprise and shutters started to slide down in his mind. A glancing thought, but of whom, she couldn't quite grasp before the woman was gone. *Yes I understand fantasies, baby. Why are you asking?*

Because I have one…

Sage's breathing was ragged by the time Caris had finished whispering her thoughts into his mind. Lids low over his eyes, his chest heaving, he slid her a narrow look and said gruffly, "You're evil."

A soft, husky chuckle escaped her lips as she bent down and kissed his forehead. "Just think. If you hurry up and get better, you just might be able to join in the fun. And of course, there is a healer en route. Kelly should be —"

"No." Sage jerked the sheet covering his lean hips up until it covered his face. "I don't need some healer sticking her hands in my head. Tell her to go back."

"Can't. We're calling our people out of the cities until we know what's going on. We've lost about twenty agents over the past few weeks." She caressed his belly through the sheet, smiling as she felt him groan. "C'mon. This is

Kelly. You can handle her. And she's gonna be here any minute."

"I don't need her healing me. I just need some rest."

"You want to keep dealing with the headache I know you have? The one I can feel just by touching you?"

Before he could answer, the door crashed open and Kelly stood there, her wide-set hazel eyes flying to the still covered Sage, her full mouth firmed into a flat, grim line, her glossy red curls spilling out from a high ponytail. The low-slung cargo pants on her hips revealed a pierced navel as she strode across the room and yanked the sheet off of Sage, glaring down at him.

"Your bedside manner leaves something to be desired, Sugar," Sage drawled up at her.

"Don't get your dick in a twist. I've seen your scrawny naked body before," she snapped, staring at him, feeling her heart tighten and tears threaten as the pain he was dealing with battered at her shields.

Sage glanced down. "I've got my shorts on. Your sensitivities aren't gonna be abused," he drawled.

"Nothing you have is likely to scare me," she sneered. Forcing the bravado up was something to keep her mind distracted as she knelt beside him and took his face in her hands. "Damn it, Sage, you know better than this. Are you trying to kill yourself?"

"No. I was trying to keep from being killed." A spasm jerked through him and his back arched up as hot healing energy jolted down his spine. He didn't mention that he could have gone to Morgan, or just stayed away. Those options really hadn't been options anyway. "Damn it, Kelly!"

The healer ignored him, focusing on the tattered, frayed passages in his mind. Stroking the pads of her fingers down his temples, Kelly swore softly. "You know better. Damn it, you know better. How many times have you bitched at me? Stupid, arrogant, bossy..." she continued to rail at him as she moved through the fine web of his mind.

Sage lay panting, gasping for air, under the deft touch of her hands. He tuned out the nagging voice with the ease of years of practice. Just before the heat of healing in his mind expanded, Sage opened his eyes and stared up at her. With an evil grin, he teased, "You're enjoying this, aren't you, baby sis?"

Kelly clenched her teeth and focused, unable to snarl at him as she flooded him, focusing on funneling her power through the link between them and shoving her psychic "hands" into his mind and repairing the tattered edges, smoothing down the grayed, burning wounds caused by excess use, and filling the emptied reserves.

Sage lost consciousness, his face going gray, his hazel eyes rolling up, body going limp. Two hands, strong and steady came up. One touched Sage's crown, stroking the thick black hair, and the other rested on Kelly's shoulder. Kelly felt the vast reserve of power as Caris opened herself up to Kelly's healing, allowing the younger woman to tap into the empath's power.

When Kelly pulled away nearly thirty minutes later, her bouncy ponytail had gone limp and wet with sweat, and her face was pale. But she was smiling tiredly and able to settle down on the floor beside Sage, stroking her fingers down his brow and studying his face with assessing eyes.

"If I got a rush like that every time I did such a healing, I would rarely have a crash." Kelly offered a crooked grin as Caris resumed her curled up spot at Sage's head.

"I seriously doubt you'd bother with filling a person's reserves when you healed them...unless it was Sage." Caris smiled easily, lifting one shoulder, laying the pad of her finger on Sage's brow and touching, testing. With a relieved smile, she looked up at Kelly. For the first time, she could touch him without tensing up. There was no screaming headache that she had to shield against, no tearing pain, no muffled feeling inside her head, nothing. He was truly resting. "He's gonna hate knowing that he relied on you this time."

Kelly grinned, a little flash of pride showing in her eyes. "He raised me to be able to take care of myself, and others. He ought to be proud of himself. If I can take care of him—" she caught the tip of her tongue between her teeth and dropped one lid in a quick wink. "Well, he did the job, well, didn't he?"

Sage had taken over the job of raising Kelly from the time he was nine, and Kelly had only been five. For five years, until Morgan had found them, he had done everything he could to be a father after their parents had been killed protecting them from those who would have destroyed them. Unlike many of their brethren, their parents had loved and protected them. It had been their grandparents who had reported them.

Sage would never forgive that. Caris knew he had done his best to shield Kelly from it, but Kelly wasn't likely to ever let it go completely. If they had been able to get to the people who had taken their parents from them—

but Morgan had ensured that would never happen. Morgan was good at that.

"Hmmm, look at what we have here. Kelly Monroe," Miguel purred from the stairs where he was leaning over the banister, his dark, Latin eyes pinned on the redhead with dark, hungry interest.

"Maguire," she corrected. Her marriage to Jed Maguire had been short-lived. But a marriage, nonetheless. The stunt pilot had died in a jetcar crash only three weeks after they had been married—very much against her brother's orders four years earlier. The twenty-five year old woman had spent nearly a year in a depressed state. She had finally come out of it when Sage had appeared on her doorstep, holding the broken, battered body of a young Firewalker girl whom he had rescued from execution.

He had grimly placed the child in Kelly's arms and said, "Are you gonna mourn yourself to death? Or join us?"

Kelly had saved the child, and never wondered why Sage had wasted precious time bringing the child to her when a teleporter almost always traveled with a healer when saving a child. He had saved this child, then brought the child to his sister, so he could save her as well.

"You are lookin' mighty fine, *amiga*." Miguel's deep baritone rolled over Kelly's skin like a silken caress and she shuddered, closing her eyes and clenching her hands in her lap, focusing on anything other than those sweet, melted chocolate eyes. "You gonna stay and play with us a while, sweet?"

"I don't play, Miguel. I stopped playing a long time ago."

Of course, playing with him held certain attractions—

Damn it. She dug her nails into her palms and opened her eyes, smiling sweetly at him. "If you're in the mood for play, you can go upstairs and join Jeza—she sounds like she needs a playmate. Me, I like my friends more grown up."

"Ouch," Miguel said mildly. One corner of his mouth curled up slowly. "Pretty girl like you ought to play from time to time, *chica*. You come find me when you're ready, Kelly. *Si*?" And then he strolled on upstairs, his tight butt catching her eye before he disappeared from view.

Chapter Ten

Jax studied the man in front of him.

He looked far too ethereal.

The white hair, the blue eyes…he looked like an angel, a heavenly creature. Until you focused on those eyes. Morgan could keep the fury in check for hours. But right now, it had escaped and fiery red flames danced behind those eyes.

Jax suspected he now knew what Morgan's gift was.

"You cannot fight a war without an army, Morgan. And it is a war you fight. You must fight it like a soldier."

Morgan's fist clenched. Slamming it on the arm of the chair, he closed his eyes. Dragged in air, blew it out.

Fighting for control, Jax suspected. Why? He didn't like hearing how totally he was being torn apart? It wasn't his fault…he was doing his best to lead these people.

"I know," Morgan snarled finally. "But I am not a fucking soldier. And I trust none who have gone into the military. They brainwash people these days. So what am I to do?"

Leaning forward, in an urgent voice, Jax said, "Lead them. But not randomly. You need to separate and assign leaders, not individual agents. You need soldiers, real soldiers."

"You are a soldier." Morgan lifted his gleaming blue eyes, the reddish flames glinting just behind the cool blue. "Are you asking to lead my people?"

Jax laughed. "No. I am no fool. You guard your people with a ferocity that even a blind man could see. But I can help." Arching a brow, Jax said, "Are you willing to allow it?"

"To keep my people alive, to protect the children, I will do whatever I must."

"And hate every second that you relinquish control, won't you?" Jax queried quietly, lifting a coppery golden brow and shaking his head.

Morgan acknowledged it with a small smile. Then he leaned forward. "You will lead half of my people, Jax. Caris, Sage, and Manuel will be your lieutenants. I'll break the people down into two groups. And I'll be keeping Dustin with me—I don't think it is wise to send him with you."

"No, I'd think not. Why do I get the feeling this should have been much harder?" Jax narrowed his eyes, studying Morgan closely.

With a grim smile, Morgan rose. "You get to break the news to Caris. She won't like knowing that she's being pulled into the thick of it all, away from her safe, quiet ranch out here in the middle of nowhere. But we need her."

Caris was so angry she couldn't breathe—her heart was racing, her head was pounding, and her body was trembling with the intensity of her fury. Her skin felt tight and itchy, and her pulse was throbbing just behind her eyes.

"You bastard." Caris felt the words squeeze through her throat as though over broken glass as she stood staring into Jax's beautiful blue eyes, that deep dreamy blue. Now almost dispassionate as he met her gaze levelly. "Don't you understand? I can't be around that many people."

"You can. You prefer not to. It is easier for you. And I do not blame you," Jax replied. Cocking his head, he stared at her, studying her closely. "You are needed, so badly. Your people suffer and die. And you all must learn to band together and fight like soldiers, like an army, a unit, not individuals. You have strong, powerful shields that you hold without a thought. Do not tell me that it would trouble you to live amongst others."

"I can't." Caris stubbornly turned away, folding her arms around her body. The suffering of so many out there, not just her brothers and sisters, but all of them. They were slowly having the life sucked out of them by the World Government, not just the Federated States, but the governing power of the planet, the one that said it sought to make life better for all of them. It mandated who could have children and who couldn't, who could have animals and who couldn't. Who could own land and who couldn't. How many children, how many animals, how much land, all to protect the planet's resources, they claimed.

Yet the planet still suffered. The people still suffered. The children who were born underground, outside the governing jurisdiction were left to fend for themselves, uncared for, unwanted, unloved. They were rife with disease, malnourished, desolate wide-eyed creatures. It was from them that many of the Firewalker children came. And Jax wanted her to go out among them.

"I won't."

"You have to." Jax stood at her back now, his heat warming her chilled body as his hands came up to rest on her shoulders and he lowered his lips to her ear. "They suffer, Caris. And will suffer more and more until you unite and fight back the way you know in your heart that you must."

"I'm not a soldier, damn it. I can't fight—"

Jax's hand slashed through the air by her head just before he turned her to face him. "I do not ask you to lift a weapon and take down your enemies, but you need to be able to face them, and stop hiding in your safe little world. You hide away from the people who need you. You are not a soldier, this I know. Leave the fighting to the soldiers, but at least do what you can, while they are doing their part."

"Do you have any idea how exhausting maintaining my shields all the time would be?" Caris felt empty, drained, battered. He was pulling her out there. No ultimatum had been delivered, no awful choice, what I say or else... Instead he had whispered of the suffering. And all but called her a coward.

None of them knew, though, what this would cost her.

Except maybe Sage. He had been around her far too long not to be aware of just how deep her particular gift— or curse—ran.

Lifting her chin, she met Jax's eyes levelly, inclining her head. Then she lowered her lashes, shutting herself off from him, closing herself in. Letting Caris out now could be deadly.

"Morgan, you can't do that to her," Sage growled, stalking into the office where Morgan was barking into the comm at some poor agent who had attempted to refuse to leave her post.

Morgan held up one hand, arching a brow.

"No. I'm not waiting." Narrowing his eyes, he focused on Morgan's face, concentrating. His head was splintered with pain by the time he was back, holding the spitting, snarling handful of Chasteen Dunn, who was still holding her comm, as though arguing with Morgan was of any use now. "She's here. Problem solved."

"Weren't you supposed to lay off the teleporting for a while?"

"Are you trying to drive Caris insane?" Sage returned sardonically. "You got any idea what it will do to her to send her out into a crowd on a mission looking for Firewalker kids?"

"Caris is stronger than she thinks. Stop trying to baby her," Morgan said flatly. He flicked his eyes to the telepath, Chasteen who was still swaying from the impromptu trip Sage had given her. "Chas, get out. Get sick somewhere else."

She stomped out in a huff as Sage glared at Morgan, blinking incredulously. Then he narrowed his eyes, furious. "Baby her? You fucking think I'm babying her? Have you ever seen what happens to that poor kid when somebody touches her unshielded? Do you have any idea how badly it drains her to hold that kind of shielding up constantly? She is a full-blown empath. Even the slightest touch causes full linking. And she doesn't even need to touch. Just looking at a person will do it. And a person in turmoil needs only to be in her vicinity to cause a link. Which means Caris will either go mad from the onslaught of emotions, or she will have to go shielded, all the damned time. She will never have time to let her guard down."

"You're exaggerating," Morgan mused, tapping his pen on the desk. "We have other empaths among us."

"You have touch-empaths. You have thought-empaths. You have healer-empaths like Kelly, and you have other agents who have a trace of what Caris has. But none have ever been like Caris. She is a touch-empath, a thought-empath with healing abilities, telepathic abilities, and the dreaming. That dreaming lets her drift into other people's dreams, sometimes even pulls her into them," Sage snapped. "You have nobody like Caris. You are throwing her out to be slaughtered and nobody knows what it will do to her, not you, and not that bloody vampire who swears he loves her so fucking much."

Jax slid into the bed behind Caris, eyeing her slim back with thoughtful eyes. The black silk that covered it made her skin glow like ivory in the dim light of the room. He wanted nothing more than to tear it from her.

But he held his hands, his temper.

He could feel a coldness radiating from her.

Not just temper, but a true coldness, as though the temperature of her body had lowered.

"Are you not well?" he murmured against her neck, cupping her in the curve of his body, stroking his hand up and down her hip. The scent of her, the feel of her flesh, the aroma of her blood flowing under her skin rushed straight to his head and hardened his cock, even as he waited for her to answer.

"I need to rest," she said woodenly.

"You are tired?"

"I will be. Forever."

Jax involuntarily clenched his hand over her hip at the flat sound of her voice, at her odd words. And something else...something that was missing. He couldn't feel her. He could no longer feel Caris. That sweet, achingly warm presence that had lingered inside his heart, his mind. She was gone, retreated inside that body, shuttered down, closed off.

"Is this my punishment?" he growled, unable to keep the threat from his voice as he spilled her onto her back, looming over her.

But Jax felt his heart rip open as he stared down into those amber colored eyes, a single tear spilling out and trickling down her cheek as Caris responded simply, "No. It's mine. My curse. My punishment."

Then she rolled back onto her side, curling up into a ball, staring into the night.

She was sulking.

Jax was certain of it.

He had thought Caris would be different than other females, but he was wrong about that apparently.

As they waited for their assigned group of people to arrive, he selected the people Caris would train, careful to keep them limited only to the empaths of the group. *I am not a blasted fool*, he thought, stalking around the perimeter of the outbuildings as Sage led his group through rigorous workouts.

Miguel had defected from the army and had established their "boot camp" as he called it. They did that physical workout every morning. Already, even after only two weeks, Jax could see much physical improvement in the health of the agents, no, the army. Their army.

Their warriors.

And Caris was still silent, still cold.

She was sitting face-to-face with a girl barely fifteen, both of them with palms up, close but not touching.

Working on shielding, Jax knew. He was familiar with the technique of it, if not the actual training. Empathy was a rare gift on his planet, and Caris was truly unique, very powerful.

Her reserves, her sources of power were near limitless, as though she drew from something other than within.

She just had to realize she was as powerful as he knew she was.

And get over her own damned pride.

Before he died of wanting her. Or the chemicals building inside his body drove him mad. He had to have her, soon.

But damned if he'd beg.

Damned if he'd ask. Never again.

Each time he had turned to her in the night of late, she had been that cold, distant, still creature. And the past week, she had slept the sleep of the dead, not even stirring when he entered the room.

"Stewing?"

The low, angry voice behind him had him closing his eyes and muffling a sigh. Shortly after Morgan and his people had left, Jax had realized that a number of the people weren't very happy with Morgan's decision. But Sage was downright furious. Oh, he was doing his job. And on the whole, he agreed, Jax suspected. But not about Caris.

"This doesn't concern you, Sage," Jax said coolly.

Sage cocked an arrogant brow as he strolled around him and braced his back against a rough wooden pillar. Studying the old, rough style of the house, Sage murmured, "Her parents knew what they were doing when they built this place for her. Her mother had a little bit of empathy. Just a little. But they knew. Caris was only six when her gifts emerged. The empathy came first. She was in school, and the school thought she was mentally retarded or insane. Even tried to have her committed. But Larelee fought the board and insisted she could school Caris at home, saying Caris was just very sensitive to people's moods, very shy. That was why, when a child came in upset it hurt her so badly. They taught her shielding, though I don't know how. But can you imagine how terrifying it would be, six years old...and the onslaught of all that emotion?"

Jax grimaced. "It would be traumatic indeed, feeling the emotions of other children."

"And the adults. You see, she walked in on a teacher being raped," Sage said flatly, straightening up and hooking his thumbs in the loops of his jeans. "I don't know the details. But she was six. And every time thereafter, once that teacher returned and saw Caris, she couldn't help but think of what had happened to her. Caris had to relive it with her."

Jax closed his eyes. "I did not know of this. But it changes nothing. Her shielding is strong. She maintains it all the time. She can function in the world and will—"

"Tell me something, oh great teacher on the mountain," Sage drawled. "Have you noticed an unusual change in Caris over the past few days?"

Jax couldn't stop the snarl that slipped past his lips, couldn't keep his teeth from flashing as his hands flexed.

Sage laughed. "I'll take that as a yes. It will only get worse. Caris has more than one way of shielding. You don't even have an inkling of how she would have to shield to deal with people on a broad spectrum, and on a daily basis. Get used to it. That's the Caris you're gonna be living with." He nodded toward the still, pale reflection of the woman Jax had fallen in love with. "She can't let herself out unless she wants to risk going mad. Not with so many unshielded people around. It would be—"

Sage...love...

The soft whispered voice wrapped around both of them, but Sage winced painfully. He slid his eyes to Caris who was now watching him carefully as she rose to her feet. *I didn't give you permission to speak of me, for me, about me. Let it go.*

Jax couldn't hear Sage's response, although he knew there was one.

Caris inclined her head gently, and then she smiled, a sad, slow smile, before she shook it negatively. *No. It just wasn't meant to be that way, babe. You win some, you lose some.*

What exactly are you talking about? Jax demanded, sliding into her end of the mental link with a deft touch.

But Caris slid out, evading him, breaking the link with a mental brush against Sage that infuriated Jax. *Thanks, babe, for caring. But I'll deal. And stay out of my business.*

Jax broke away, furious, seething.

She would tell him what he wanted to know.

Chapter Eleven

Brooding, angry, plotting, he waited until later in the day before he moved in on her. When he saw that she was weary, but not to the point that she would drop exhausted the moment she hit the bed.

"Why are you so exhausted? Are you taking ill?" he asked cordially as he led her away from the group, his hand splayed protectively over her back as he guided her to their room. Anni had cooked dinner for her and the scents of it wafted appetizingly from the hallway even before he opened the door.

"No," she said shortly. "I am not ill. I am not taking ill."

"You sleep twelve hours every day. That is not the normal pattern for an adult human."

"Studying up on the humans now, are we?" she asked dryly as she slid past him into the room, narrowly eyeing the lone table setting, the candlelight. "What the hell is this?"

"Dinner, love," he murmured against her neck.

"Fine." She shrugged his hands away and moved off, leaving him standing there staring at her. Taking a deep breath, closing his hands into fists and then flexing them, he reminded himself there was a purpose to tonight. And spanking her sweet little ass wasn't it.

She picked through the food while standing, settling on the bowl of soup, which she ate while roaming the room and ignoring him, occasionally going back to the table to munch on bread or sip at the wine. When she finished, she set it down and turned, facing him and folding her arms across her chest. "Now what?"

"Eat the rest," he growled as he struggled to rein in his temper. Oh, she was pushing it.

"I'm not hungry. I'm tired, and I still have work to do. There's tons of clothes to wash now that you've invaded my home and let nearly a hundred people onto my land without my permission. And even more on the way. Housing is being built, I'm told. Without my permission—" her voice broke and she closed her eyes, swallowed. "On my land. And what the fuck am I supposed to do about it? There's nothing I can do. Nothing."

Jax reached for her as she turned, only to have her jerk away. "Don't. I don't want you touching me right now," she hissed. "Damn it, you helped him do this to me. Morgan knows, damn it, part of him knows what this will do to me, and he doesn't care. And you helped him."

Jax heard none of it though, he only saw his mate, his woman, pulling away. That wasn't allowed. That wasn't acceptable. Fisting one hand in her hair, the other an iron clamp around her belly, he pinned her against the wall and licked her neck, growling softly, "You are mine, Caris...remember?"

His hand slid down her belly, under the loose tie of her pants, cupping her in his hand. He pushed one thick finger between the bare lips of her sex, the scant dampness there resisting his entrance as he rocked his cock against her ass. "Mine...to feed on, to fuck, to love...do not ever pull away from me." He pulled his finger out and pushed it back in, shuddering as a wave of her sweet cream greeted him this time, easing his passage.

"I'd never place you in direct harm. You will trust me. And you will tell me what you were speaking of with Sage. Or you will pay..." he whispered in soft sensual threat as he licked a trail down her neck, feeling a long slow shudder rack her body. Gripping the fragile, gaily colored, flower-patterned pink pants at her hips, he tore them away, then went back to rocking his cock against her ass. He took two handfuls of her bright pink shirt and rent it away, leaving her naked, her hair spilling down her pale back in a golden river of silk, her entire body shuddering.

"Will you tell me, as I worship your body?" he asked, fondling a breast with one hand while he tormented the hard nub of her clit with the other hand. "Or do I make you tell me?"

"My conversations are my own," she said roughly, breathing in ragged pants, reaching up to knock his hands away, only to be caught up against him, her arms pinned against her chest. Jax breathed in the sweet jasmine and vanilla scent of her, the feel of her against him, and worried about the coolness of her body.

"You feel too cold against me. I want to know why. If you are not ill, then tell me why you feel so cold."

"Kiss my ass," she rasped, jerking her head aside as he craned around to buss his lips against hers.

Slowly, he turned her stiff body around in his arms and carried her over to the bed, tossing her down on it and looming over her, waiting to see if she would try to run. Her eyes, that peculiar golden brown, the same color as her hair, met his unyieldingly, and she lifted that stubborn, arrogant chin.

A smile tugged at his lips even as the challenge and refusal in her gaze made his blood boil, made his heart pound in fast, heavy beats, calling to the predator that he kept leashed inside. "I'm going to fuck you mercilessly, for every time you refuse me, Caris. Until you scream my name over and over, until you cannot think for want of me. Be careful that you do not ask for more than you can handle. I will take you everywhere you have ever dreamed of…and I will make you want it, I will make you crave it."

"Oh, go screw yourself," she snorted, rolling onto her belly and starting to crawl away.

Jax stared hungrily at the exposed ass, and lunged, pinning her under him, between his body and the bed, raking his teeth down her neck as he caught her arms, stretching them over her head and gripping her wrists in one hand. Rising to his knees, he tore at the material of his shirt, scowling at the unfamiliar fasteners and shredding it, tossing the torn material to the side. Holding onto two longer strips, he released Caris' wiggling, furious body, and flipped her around on the bed so that her head was up by the posts.

Before she could open her mouth to hiss at him, he had one wrist neatly, firmly but safely restrained, with her flat on her belly. He was reaching for the other when she snaked onto her back and scissored out with her leg, delivering a damaging blow right to his balls. Jax doubled over, gasping, falling back and wishing he hadn't taken to wearing the human's clothing. His light armor would have protected him from that blow. By the suns…

And the little witch was fast. He was slowly rising from his bent position, not thirty seconds later, when she was nearly through the first series of intricate knots. Bending low over her, he ran one hand up the length of her back, then down before lifting his hand and delivering a sound smack to the firm, toned flesh of her ass. "Do that again, beloved, and I shall turn this pretty tail of yours red as roses, red as the soft flesh of your sweet pussy, do you understand?" he purred, as he caught her free hand and forced it down to the mattress, tying it to the other post.

Then he bent low and murmured, "I'll fuck that virgin ass this night. That shall be your punishment, and your reward for telling me what I wish to know. And pleasure for both of us. You will know a painful pleasure like none you have ever experienced. And you will crave more of it."

"Go fuck yourself, Jax," she hissed, jerking her head away from his soft, crooning voice.

"Tell me no, and I shall go," he offered. "Scream for help, if you are truly frightened."

"I am not afraid of you," she hissed indignantly, totally forgetting the first words he had whispered against her cheek. He stared into the golden fire of her eyes, and saw nothing but challenge. "And I don't owe you any damn explanation. Now untie me and leave me the hell alone."

Jax smiled, a hot, slow curl of his lips. "You did not say no." Pulling back, he jerked her to her knees and used his thumbs to spread the pouting lips of her sex. Staring hungrily at the glistening wet flesh, his aching fangs descended from their sheaths as he lowered his head and licked her pussy. He eagerly probed the damp folds with his tongue, listening to the scream she muffled against her arm.

The sweet, sweet beckon of her blood filled the air as he pushed his tongue further into her passage and reached between her thighs, circling his finger around her clit until she was shuddering and quaking under his hands.

"Scream for me..." he whispered into her mind. Only to be blocked. He pushed against those shields as he had done before, expecting to feel them fall, but they didn't. Ramming himself against her mentally, he shifted lower, flipping to his back and catching her clit gently between his teeth so he could finger-fuck her as he worked against the shields surrounding her heart, her soul—Caris.

"You hold yourself away from me," he whispered, pulling back, murmuring it against the silken naked flesh of her mound. "I will not allow this. Open yourself to me."

"This is what you forced me into," she said, her voice quivering as he pushed two thick fingers deep inside the slick, wet channel of her cleft. Jax lashed down the urge to drive his cock inside her until she screamed his name, until those thick impenetrable walls fell in shatters around them and he could warm himself in the fire of her soul...but she was so much colder now than he.

"I will break down those damned walls," he growled, sliding out from between her firm sweet thighs and rolling off the bed, staring down at her exposed, lifted ass, running his tongue over his fangs before stalking over to the bedside table and jerking it open. "You will scream out my name. You will yield to me. You will tell me what I need to hear."

"What about what I need?" Caris snarled, whipping her head around and glaring at him, her cheek pressed against the pillow as she tracked him with her eyes.

"I know what you need. I also know what you want. To be alone, safe and alone." He opened the small glass jar of lubricant, the rich scent wafting to his nostrils as he took a generous amount and stroked it over his cock, staring at her as he did. "Safe and alone, that is what you want. And need? You need this...me."

"Want... You think I enjoy being away from people all the time?" she said thickly, staring at his cock, almost as though entranced. Her eyes followed his hand up and down as he stroked himself, and Jax closed his eyes, enjoying the warm slippery, silken feel of the lubricant under his hand, imagining the way her tight little ass was going to feel, in just seconds. The hard, rigid length of his cock jerked under his hand and he opened his eyes, closing the distance between them, moving behind her as she tried to close her legs. He wedged one broad thigh between hers as he mounted her.

"Tell me what I want to know, open yourself to me, and I will lay you down and worship you as though you were a queen," he whispered, lowering his lips to her back.

"Kiss my ass," she snarled furiously, jerking away from his touch, trying to twist out of his reach.

"I'd rather fuck it," he replied, slapping it lightly before probing the tender pink hole with his slick, lubed finger and pushing it in even as she gasped for breath. "You will scream my name."

"No..."

In response, Jax pushed a second finger inside the snug passage and groaned as it writhed and spasmed around him, struggling to accommodate him. Pumping his fingers in and out, he settled on his heels, watching her, as she started to rock back against him.

That was when he pulled his fingers away and gripped her hip with one hand, and his cock in the other. Pressing the broad, ruddy head against the tender pink hole, Jax pushed deep, slowly, watching as it flowered open around him and listening as Caris sobbed. Her breath was coming in deep ragged pants, the scent of her blood rising and becoming thicker on the air.

Pulling out minutely, he pushed slowly back in as a flood of her cream washed down to coat his sac and fill the air, making him ravenous. "You're hot...finally your body warms," he crooned. "I can taste your want on the air, hear how fast your heart pounds. Scream for me, let me hear it."

Caris shuddered, her spine bowing down, her hands closing into fists as she jerked against the cloth strips binding her wrists and he pushed deeper and deeper inside her. The tight, hot, silken grip of her ass hugged him, writhing around him, had him gritting his teeth and arching his head back, his hair falling down his back, the ends of his hair caressing his spine, his every last nerve ending hyper-sensitized...

The scent of her blood...whipping his head up, he stared at her, the way she had her head turned, her silken, amber and gold locks covering her face as she squirmed under his slow, deep possession. Pushing her hair aside, he snarled as he saw her teeth sinking into her arm, smothering her moans in her throat, as she shuddered under his hands.

"Damn it, Caris," he swore, pulling out and surging forward, spreading the cheeks of her bottom open and staring down, watching as her eyes flew open then fluttered closed. Reaching around her hip, he pinched her clit as he started to shaft her deeply, burying his cock inside the tight, silky, virgin passage completely as the musk of her need filled the air. The scent of her blood and her body drove him insane.

"Scream...scream..."

She shuddered, she shook, and she sobbed against her arm, but she didn't scream. Reaching down, he twined his fingers in her hair and tugged her head just slightly, until she pulled her mouth from her arm. Jax swore heatedly when he saw the bruised, red bite mark on her arm, drops of blood trickling down her smooth ivory flesh. With a savage growl, he ripped the cloth binding her, sliding his hands around her waist and lifting her up against him. Craning his head around to lick the bleeding wound he wrapped his arms around her and swiveled his hips against the soft curves of her butt.

"Do not ever mark yourself, Caris," he said, pressing his cheek to hers, shuddering as she started to clench and spasm around his cock. "Do not do it. Scream for me, give it to me…"

Her eyes opened and he heard the catch in her breath as he started to jackhammer his hips against hers, ears pricked for the scream as she started to come. His cock jerked and he started pumping wave after wave of come into her willing, tight little ass.

A soft, muffled sob was the only sound that left her lips. And when Jax forced his heavy lids open to stare into her eyes, she turned her head away as she came in a long, pulsating wave around his cock.

Stubborn little wench, Jax swore hotly as he lowered her body to the bed, bracing his hands on her hips before gently pulling out.

Flipping her onto her back, he sprawled between her thighs and spread the lips of her sex with his thumbs before lifting his eyes to stare at her over the length of her still quivering body. "So sweet…" he muttered, inhaling the heady scent of warm, hungry woman as he lowered his mouth to her pussy. "Scream, scream my name. Tell me you love me..."

Stiffening his tongue he probed the folds hungrily, moving up and flicking it against her clit. Her thighs stiffened against his cheeks, and she arched up, gasping and sobbing for air, whimpering deep in her throat. "Jax, stop," she finally whimpered.

"Scream," he growled. "I want to hear you scream my name."

Instead, she sank her sharp, white little teeth into her full lower lip as she arched up against his mouth, shuddering her way through another climax as he started to work two fingers in and out of her sheath.

Jax groaned and pulled his mouth away from her sweet, wet cleft and rested his head on her quivering belly. His back bowed up as he forced his fangs back up into their sheaths, reining his body under control, even though his hunger still gnawed at his belly, his cock, his soul. "You belong to me—I'll hear my name on your lips again. Our souls are one," he murmured, stroking one hand up and down her hip.

Long moments later, he moved away and lay on his side, drawing her up into the cradle of his body, stroking his thumb up and down the curve of her hip as the shudders racking her body slowly faded.

Into the silence, she whispered, "Our souls can't be one. Your soul doesn't know mine."

Chapter Twelve

Caris glanced up at Anni as the younger woman slid into the room where she was practicing with Rebecca. Becca was fifteen, sassy, smart, and a projecting empath. She could project her emotions onto any one person...or persons. The problem was that she couldn't control it when she was too angry, too scared, too hurt.

She had been twelve years old and listening to her parents fight when her gift emerged. Becca hadn't meant to hurt anybody, but she had. The backlash of her emerging gift had destroyed her mother's mind. Granted, it was no big loss. The selfish bitch had never wanted anything but to be free of her family, her job, her obligations...everything.

Her father, once he recovered from the shock, had taken Becca and fled. He had met up with Morgan two years ago, but the poor, loyal father had died during one of the many attacks against the Firewalkers. He had taken a strike aimed for his daughter, and died with a smile on his face, knowing she was in good hands.

The trauma in Becca's background resulted in uncontrolled bursts that sometimes resulted in chaos wherever Becca went. Hence, her being with Caris. This girl was going to learn basic shielding, though she'd never need to learn shielding on the level that Caris had to shield. She didn't need to filter out all the random bits and pieces that could drive Caris to the extreme.

No, what Becca had to do was learn not to let her own inner torment spill out onto others.

She was actually getting better.

So far, Caris had only felt the urge to wail at Becca's loss of control once or twice today.

Usually she was a bawling mess on the inside within minutes of dealing with this child.

But she adored her. She was a feisty fighter with a sunny disposition, when Caris wasn't forcing her mind back to the dark and dreary things that Becca would rather forget.

Which left Caris open to other emotions, some random and indefinable. Others clearer…like the rage and confusion and discontent from Jax. And the feelings from Anni. Very clear, very focused. Her dark golden eyes were troubled. Her spiky black hair was in disarray as though she had been running her hands through it, and often.

And the thoughts from her mind…"already"…? over and over. As Caris worked Becca through another basic shielding technique, she glanced over at Anni to see her slide a glance toward the door before hugging herself, her gloved black hands rubbing up and down her arms as though she were cold.

Poor Caris, he just doesn't get it…

Oh, shit.

"Becca, I think we'll call it quits for now. You've done a great job the past few days. You deserve a break," Caris said, keeping her voice even once Becca had managed to mount the basic shield, grounding, focusing, thinking of solid stone walls…only this one had a window. A window that saw Caris. And Caris was allowed to feel all of Becca's emotions. This gift of Becca's could possibly be a weapon, if they trained it right.

Caris wasn't sure yet.

Right now, she allowed herself a brief moment to bathe in the glow of the girl's happiness. She was so desperate to find some relief, some kind of help with this burden of hers.

But once the girl dashed out, Caris slid her eyes to Anni, golden amber meeting the darker gold of the younger woman's. Caris kept her face impassive. Anni, no matter what else she was, would always be a predator first. Her first instinct would be to attack, to strike out. To draw blood.

And Caris was sorely afraid that if she let the girl see how despondent she was becoming, Anni just might try to strike out at the source of Caris' distress.

Not that Jax would ever hurt her.

But that was the last thing they needed right now. One more stress in the already overburdened new army. The word brought a hot ball of rage to Caris' belly and she had to tamp it down as her heart started to pound, calling to the predator in the room. Anni's brows arched and her nose twitched, her tongue sliding out to dampen her lips.

"Out with it, kitten. I heard it the moment you came in. Something's up. What has the little tiger so upset?"

Anni forced a smile and haughtily said, "I prefer to be called a panther, thank you."

It was more appropriate, with the black hair, the all black clothing Anni loved to wear. Caris grinned and said, "Maybe we should get you a black tail to wear. Start calling you *el leopardo nigra,* or something cool like that.

But that isn't what has you stalking around here, babe. What gives?"

Anni dropped into a boneless little heap, reclining against Caris companionably. "You were one of the first people to make me feel like something other than a freak, you know that, Caris?"

"You aren't a freak, sweetie. You were born this way for a reason. We all were. We'll know that reason in time." Caris wrapped her arm around Anni's slim shoulders and bent low over her, hugging her, resting her forehead against Anni's head. "We've done a lot of good, saved a lot of children's lives. Even helped the fools that condemn us."

"I know. You're the one that made me understand that. You see what's inside us. You feel it. You make us understand it. Even when you don't want to, even when it hurts you. Sage knows that. I know it, to some extent. I saw how badly it tore you up a few times—especially with me, I could hear you. I know how messed up I was, that first summer, after I went crazy—"

Anni's voice broke and Caris could feel the blackness of guilt swallowing her up. "Anni, don't do this to yourself. You were attacked, baby."

"The first time. Yes. But then—"

"No buts. The first time you were attacked and you were just a teenager. Barely hit puberty and you were defending yourself when this change started on you. Between that Changing and you almost being raped, plus having to kill to defend yourself, it's no wonder you went a little mad."

"My madness took the lives of five men. Some of those men probably didn't deserve to die. And my madness almost pulled you with me." Rising to a seated position with that smooth, easy grace, folding her legs under her, Anni focused her dark eyes on Caris' face and said, "It could happen to you. I know that. You fear it as well. I can smell it, feel it. Am I right?"

Caris inclined her head. "I don't know if it could happen. I don't think it's completely farfetched," she murmured, lifting one shoulder absently. Anni's stare had her pinned in place, unable to tear her eyes away. It was a predator's stare, like a tiger's, or a panther's. A hypnotic, enticing, deadly gaze that pulled you in and under. "And yes, I do fear it. After what happened with you, and some others, I've realized just how deeply I can connect with others. Sometimes, entirely too deeply. The more traumatized a child is, the quicker that child can pull me in. The places I've been pulled into aren't places anybody can go to follow me."

Anni made a mewling sound deep in her throat, and lowered her head, now the hurt little kitten as she crawled over to Caris. It startled her at times, how animal-like this woman could act. It didn't help, though, that after Anni had gone a little mad, she had fled to the wilds in Alaska, going to ground in one of the few wild refuges left on the planet. She had lived for months in solitude while her twin brother Dustin tried to find her, and ended up in Morgan's hands.

"Anni, what's happened? What is going on?"

"Morgan called," Anni whispered roughly. "There's a rally against us in Des Moines. They have a child, one of ours, a girl. But some uncontacted rebels will be there. He wants you to talk to the rebels and try to bring them over. Jax agreed. Sage and he are going over the plans now.

"They're sending you into a throng, Caris. An angry mob."

"Sage wouldn't make plans about that without telling me," Caris said faintly as black dots started to spin in front of her eyes.

"He doesn't know. Jax and Morgan refused to tell him. They want him focused. He's not been himself since he had the collapse, and well, Sage is madder than hell about even having to work with Jax right now. He has to focus, though, so he's pushing it aside. You'll be sent in after he's gone after the girl," Caris murmured. "Jax and I are to go with you and work as your backup, your bodyguard. And Sage is taking the girl to Morgan's group for healing…to keep him away from here, until you're back."

Caris stood up slowly, feeling her skin stretch tight and hot, then go all cold, all within the span of heartbeats. Her head was spinning, black dots rushing in on her vision and she was pretty damn certain she would have vomited, if she had eaten anything in the past twelve hours.

Her lashes lowered over her eyes as she sensed Jax drawing closer. A tensing of power around the area told her what she had feared. Sage had just teleported away. Fuck…the one person she could have used with her. *Maybe I shouldn't have been so close-lipped lately.*

Anni was dangerous. Downright deadly, when she was angered. A bloodlust ran in her veins, highly refined senses, night sight, all the features that made the deadly cats deadly…

But Anni couldn't help Caris protect herself.

Sage could have.

Lowering her forehead to the glass, Caris braced herself as Jax opened the door and came through. Ice flowed through the room, coating everything within as the vampire studied Anni. "It would seem my presence here is unnecessary — both of you seem to already know what we need to do," he mused.

Every muscle seemed to draw tighter and tighter as he spoke. Caris forced herself to breathe slow and deep, relaxing the tensed muscles in her body, trying to slow her rabbiting thoughts. I can handle this...it's been ten years since I last went out into a mass of people and I wasn't prepared for what could happen.

I can handle this.

I can handle this.

"Caris, must you persist in ignoring me?" Jax growled.

Anni was resting her chin on her knees when Caris turned around slowly, meeting those dark golden eyes for one long moment.

"She isn't ignoring you, oh great vampire," Anni mocked lightly, arrogantly, so very un-Anni-like. "She heard you loud and clear."

"Don't, Anni," Caris said softly, shaking her head as Jax's eyes flickered and his fangs started to slide down. She returned her gaze to Jax and said, "Throttle down, Chief. You wanted the command of a bunch of American rebels. You had no clue what you were asking for, slick. Anni just gave you a taste. We are not like the people you are used to leading, Jax."

"Anni, you will never do this again. However you heard, whatever you were doing, stop doing it," Jax said, turning to stare at Anni with cold eyes.

Anni laughed, rolling onto her belly, and kicking her feet in the air, crossing her ankles. Her dainty fangs flashed as she smiled at them. "Should I cut off my ears? Plan on never being within a hundred feet of the house? So sorry, sweetie, I can't help what I overhear. This was just something that caught my attention."

"Anni's got the ears of a cat, love," Caris said silkily. "She'd have to pretty much vacate the premises altogether to avoid possibly overhearing something. She can't help having that hearing."

"Enough, Caris." Aiming his chilly eyes her way, Jax said, "I assume you know what you are going to be doing, then? You realize how much you are needed. You can no longer deny this."

"No. I've never bothered to deny that I'm needed. I've even gone out from time to time and done exactly this. However, I prefer to plan and do it myself, my way."

"I'm aware of how you've always done it. With Sage, and Sage only. No more than a handful of times in the past, bringing in only a handful of people. We need to recruit strong leaders, not just the troubled children," Jax said, his voice softening. "I know how to fight battles."

Caris made a tiny sound, muffled deep in her chest and walked away. "I'll be waiting by the ALTV," she said over her shoulder.

Anni rolled to her feet in a smooth, liquid motion, her eyes on Caris. She waited until Caris had moved out of sight before she looked back at Jax. "You may know how to fight a battle but you don't understand the weapons you hold."

Sage smoothed the sleeping teen's hair away from her face. This one had been almost an adult. The state of

Montana was still a little leery of killing children. No matter that they could spin fire in their hands or not. Well, this one had been a mind reader and speaker.

Not even a terribly uncommon gift. Some people even still believed in psychics.

What was really wrong was that she could control other people through their minds. And she had tried to use her gift to convince a local warden to let go the entire population of Firewalkers.

Too large an order for such a young warrior.

She had almost succeeded.

Almost…which is why they had decided to kill her. Publicly. And with her drugged up to boot.

"She'll be a good hand to have on our side," Morgan had said. "We need more like her. Too damn bad we can't get Caris to act like this kid did."

"This kid doesn't take the emotions of others inside her," Sage had said shortly. Frustrated and tired of trying to explain the same thing over and over to Morgan, he turned and pinned him with an angry glare. "Caris gets too caught up in the emotions without a blocker between her and those she's trying to help. She has to lower her shields when she's trying to speak to that many people. It weakens her shields. And the volatile emotions of the suffering are her weakness. She can't fight it. Anni almost destroyed her.

"That's why I go out with her. I block and filter what comes through to her. Without that, she stands the risk of getting swallowed up," Sage said, turning away.

"You're just hypothesizing, right?" Morgan asked.

"No. We've tried. We've been testing her gifts fairly regularly. Hell, how in the world do you think we ended up such good friends? How do you think we know each other so well? We've been working on pounding this thing out for the past ten years and so far, this is the only way it works."

"What do you mean, swallowed up? She gets sick for a while? Drained?"

Sage's lips canted up in a cruel, cold smile. "No. I mean go insane. That barrage of emotion, if she can't filter it away, will drive her mad. And too much could likely kill her."

Morgan growled out, "Why are you the only two who know that?"

"Because it's her gift. It's her choice…and I'm the only one she trusts enough to filter for her. And with good reason. You'd throw her to the dogs, if it suited your purpose," Sage sneered.

The soft, simple "Fuck," Morgan uttered made Sage's blood run cold.

As he turned and met Morgan's eyes, Sage felt his world start to grow even darker. "No. You didn't. You said you'd wait."

"She's at the rally."

Caris kept up a partial shield, filtering out the way Sage had always done. She moved among the people who were still trying to figure out what in the hell had happened, homing in easily on those who were brothers in arms, rebels fighting alone. Three refused to fight any other way.

But more…more wanted to come to the safety of numbers. Anni had the job of herding them to different areas where they'd get information on where to go and how they'd hook up.

So far, so good.

Until now… Caris froze as a security officer stopped in front of her, watching in numb terror as two men grabbed another man who was trying to protect a small child. A child who had the odd glowing eyes of the Firewalker blood. The child was too young to have learned to stop the glowing. He had brought her out. Or she had slipped out.

The security officer was terrified. Furious. At…the men who held the arms of the child. The security officer wore the standard eye shields of the department, but Caris would be willing to bet near anything—

Too fucking many people around. *If I stop them now, I get caught and I can't help anybody else. Damn it! But the baby…*

Blackness, despair, rage, heartbreak…the whirlpool of emotion was pulling at Caris' mind as she started toward the child and the father as somebody moved out of the crowd, drawing an illegal gun, several hundred years old. Standard weapon for those who hated the Firewalkers. Caris lunged, evading Jax's hands, twisting away from him and bellowing even as the security officer drew her psilgun.

But it was too late.

The father lay on the ground, bleeding from a ragged hole in his chest, a sickening whistle coming from the wound. His eyes wheeled to the girl who was screaming in anger, terror, shock, as her skin started to glow red.

"Vatalini…"

Caris seized the child and dropped her first layer of shields, throwing an external one around the child, the security officer and her seething bodyguard. Everyone else around them went numb with the terror the girl was suffering, the pain the father felt.

Anni was moving through them like a feline shadow, hissing as one woman who had been hurling obscenities tried to clutch at Anni in terror, pleading for help. "Like you helped them, you mean?" Anni spat, her lip curled up in disgust.

Caris cupped the father's cheek in one hand as she held the girl against her side. "Don't fight the pain, not for her sake. I'm a stranger to you, I know. But I'm like she is. I'll watch over her and protect her, teach her. You have a touch of what she will become. You know I speak the truth."

"Vatalini," he rasped, reaching up with a trembling hand to touch her cheek.

The little girl flung herself down to hug him, wrapping her frail little arms around his neck, sobbing his name. "Daddy, daddy, please, get up. I won't disappear again, never, never…"

"Sweet, this isn't…your…fault. Love you. Listen to the pretty lady. She'll take you now," he breathed against her hair, his darkening eyes meeting Caris' over the child's head.

Caris felt the madness pushing at her, the child's terror, fear, and the guilt…oh, the guilt, *bad Vay-Vay was bad and now see Daddy?*

Don't! You can't do this now, she told herself.

"Damn it all, Caris, you cannot rush in like this," Jax rasped, snarling as one man attempted to shove the veil of fear aside. *I thought she had more sense than this and now I lose her*—his mind, his gut, his heart, all a swirling morass of grief and fear and rage.

Caris throttled down and focused. *Sage...where are you?*

The familiar touch on his mind was at once both welcome and hated. Her voice was full of determination, focus, rage. And a summons. Caris never summoned him. She needed him—enough to reach out and touch his mind, blindly, without thinking, something that for Caris was too painful, too intense, too clear. Even his mind—he could block and filter the thoughts she could touch—was far too intense for an empath of Caris' ability.

Sage lifted glowing hazel eyes and met Morgan's. "She's calling me. And she's in trouble. Caris never calls for me," he said simply. Shaking his head grimly, he said bluntly, "If she didn't need me, I'd kill you for this."

Morgan's eyes narrowed and he said, "You need to be careful with what you say, Sage."

"Screw being careful, Morgan. And fuck you," Sage said, stepping back. He closed his eyes and focused on Caris' face, feeling the vortex opening up around him even as Morgan started to speak. It didn't matter.

Finding Caris mattered.

Saving his best friend mattered.

The ground solidified under his feet and he felt the onslaught of grief, and wanted to fall to his knees sobbing. The wails that filled the air around him told him Caris was losing control. They'd have blood on the ground from people trying to cut their pain out if she didn't stop. As he forced a shield between him and her weapon, he moved up behind her, feeling his heart break as he saw the struggling child in her arms. Caris was rocking back and forth, trying to calm the little girl, who was fighting to get back to the man who lay gasping out his last breaths on the ground.

"Daddy! Somebody help my daddy!"

"Baby, he's been hurt too badly...I don't have that kind of gift," Caris whispered. "I can't heal that kind of hurt. I don't know of a healer who could undo that kind of damage."

There was no way the girl could understand. But maybe Caris was trying to convince herself, Sage mused as he knelt behind them and lay his palm on Caris' back. "I'm here, babe. We have to get you away before these people go insane. Before you do."

Sage was getting ready to do just that when both he and Caris sensed the little snap of somebody's control breaking. Golden amber and dark hazel gazes lifted to the security officer, clad in the somber gray uniform, her eyes inscrutable behind her shades, her face pale and grim...she moved like a wraith to the man who was no longer breathing on the ground.

"I'm sorry...I'm such a coward," she whispered, laying a hand on the hole in his chest. With a hand that glowed, light pulsing from it, light blazing from behind the standard issue shades that still covered her eyes, she touched him. Closing her eyes, she said, "Don't listen to the people who are calling you. Listen to my voice, stay with your daughter, man. Stay here with us."

"There's no way—" Sage murmured, shaking his head, hair tumbling into his eyes, his throat spasming as the young girl in Caris' arms screamed "Daddy, come back!"

"He's not gone," Caris whispered, cocking her head, stroking the child's hair and shushing her. "There is some part of him still here."

"You need a damned good healer…"

Jax appeared at their side. "We need to get out of here. Get Caris away. Now," Jax growled at Sage as Sage uncurled from his crouch, turning to the vampire with cold, blank eyes.

Fury raced through Sage as he faced the vampire. "You were supposed to protect her, not throw her into the lion's den. Now you want me to take care of her ass?"

Jax snarled, his fangs glinting as his arm flashed out, but Sage merely blinked and the hand slammed into a wall only a millimeter in front of Sage's face. Snapping hazel eyes met the cold blue of the vampire's and Sage drawled, "Do you really think I'd wait here with her unprotected? I would never leave her unprotected. I know how vulnerable she is — unlike you and our fearless leader."

"Sage." The soft, whisper of his name from Caris belied the calm expression on her face. She was shattering inside. "Let it go. He didn't know. They wouldn't believe me until they saw it."

Sage stared at Jax until a piercing scream from outside the circle of despair caught his attention. "No, I can't take it…" a woman sobbed.

"Caris, they are losing it." Sage turned away from Jax, kneeling in front of Caris and meeting her eyes, holding her gaze. "I'm here now. You won't feel any more from them. I can't stop what is inside now, but you won't feel anymore. Let them go before anything happens."

He saw the terror in her eyes, the anguish and the guilt for the suffering she was inflicting even as she let them go. The screams and moans of anguish turned into rage and hatred. Closing his hands over her ears, he muffled the sounds and focused on her mind. *Don't focus on the sound…focus on her, the baby, on Jax and how furious he is with me right now. See the look on his face?*

A muffled sound, between a giggle and a sob left her lips. *How can I not see it? If he could tear down that wall, he'd kill you. He'd be sorry later, but he'd kill you. He didn't know you could do this. He wants to know why. And he wants to squeeze your throat until your eyeballs pop out.*

He's graphic about what he wants, huh? Sage teased. *Don't you think he's overreacting a little though? I'm just trying to help…*

You're trying to cause trouble like you always do. Caris took a deep breath, closing her eyes, focusing, or trying to. Sage could still feel the wildness inside her. She was close to breaking. He had to get them out of here. But he couldn't leave—not even for a minute.

"Jax, I need them all next to me," he said flatly, not taking his hands from Caris' face.

Jax growled under his breath but moved to the healer who said, "I can't take my hands from him."

"We stay here, we die."

Sage tossed her a flicker of a look before returning his focus to Caris and flashing a smile. "Hang in there, babe. Watch me pull a rabbit out of my hat." He dropped a slow teasing wink and sent a long-cherished memory, that first time they came together, and watched her blush.

Behind him, he heard Jax say, "Silence, lady. You heard Sage. We stay, we die. Do you want your sacrifice to go to waste? The child to die? Walk at his side. I will carry him. Bloody *piquan* that he is, Sage is a wise man in some ways and he has some plan to get us out of here. Now be silent and continue."

Sage watched as the glowing bright light came closer and closer, and said, "Touching, Jax. I need all of you touching me."

"You do not want me able to touch you, Sage," Jax purred.

"You want to see your lady sane, Jax. That is what I'm trying to do. So shut the hell up and get closer." He dropped the shield between him and the vamp and felt the cooler, bigger body move up on the other side and waited for Anni to curl up at his back. The healer placed one hand on his shoulder, gently laying one of the dying man's hands on Sage's knee. Sage smiled gently at the girl in Caris' arms and held his arm's out to Caris. "Come on, baby. Let's see if I can do this. Open up that amazing soul of yours. I need more than I have inside me," he murmured, drawing her to his chest and murmuring against her cheek as they cradled the girl between them.

Falling into the shining, golden reserves that was Caris' power, Sage drew it inside him, breathing it in, shuddering and feeling his skin draw tight, his heartbeat racing as he built up what he needed before focusing.

Dropping the shields between him and the crowd, Sage drew upon the focal points of those touching him...and flung them into the vortex. The pull of the added strain weighed him down. Sage could feel it, fought against the need to stop and rest, something deadly in the vortex, the gap between here and there.

He crashed into the hard floor of Caris' house and fell back against Anni, into her arms as they landed, shuddering and dragging air into his starving lungs. His head was burning from the inside as his shields protecting Caris exploded and fell to pieces. She started screaming.

The child flung herself at her father, wailing his name and Anni leaped, pulling her into her arms, whispering gently, "No, lamb. Not yet. Let the good lady help him first."

And still Caris screamed, her eyes blind with terror, with fear, with guilt, as the emotions that filled the room filled her.

Sage rolled to his knees and crawled to her, reaching out to touch her, to re-establish the shields.

But before he could, Jax had cradled her in his arms, calling her name beseechingly, his eyes panic stricken, wide and stark with terror. Sage could feel a gray oblivion tugging at his mind, but he shoved it back. Unless Kelly or Ari made it here, he was the only one who had dealt with her when she was like this.

Moving gingerly to her side, Jax knelt in front of her and placed one hand on her heart, the other on her cheek. Probing inside the desperate, terrified woman, he stole some of the power that resided there, tapping into it and forcing a shield between her panic-stricken screams and the chaotic emotions that surrounded them, inflicting their madness on her.

Jax tore his eyes away from Caris' face and asked roughly, "What is going on? What has happened to her?"

"Caris cannot be exposed to such raw emotion, Jax. It will drive her insane. We tried to tell y'all this, but I guess you didn't want to hear." His eyes smoldering, he met the vampire's gaze and said, "Hopefully her screams won't be the last thing you ever hear from her."

"Sage—"

But whatever the vampire was going to say was lost as he sank into the dark, tortured recesses of Caris' mind.

Chapter Thirteen

Jax stroked his hand through Caris' golden-amber hair, pressing his lips to her brow, searching through his soul for some distant link to her. Nothing…nothing that he recognized anyway. Darkness, despair, wild, unending pain—that he recognized. But nothing of her, nothing that felt right.

When an unrecognizable force shoved at his mind, Jax threw it away and hovered protectively around Caris, waiting desperately for Sage to do something.

I am trying, damn it. Let me in, a dry, aggravated voice said. *You have a link to her – I need that, something to bring her back to herself. Now damn it, vampire, let me in.*

Lifting his eyes, Jax blinked, throwing off the effects of that powerful voice that had echoed within his mind, through his shields. Meeting Sage's eyes, he dropped the shields and tried to steady himself as the power of the teleporter rolled through him.

*By the Suns…by the Holy One's blood…*Jax thought, clenching his teeth as his head fell back, the veins in his neck bulging out. If he had been standing, he would have fallen. The power was Caris', borrowed, he could scent it. But the ability within Sage was tremendous. And he had thought teleporting was the man's true gift.

Relax, I won't hurt you. Much.

Jax could feel him riffling through his memories, his soul, his mind, as though Sage were searching through a box for a long lost token. Amusement spread from Sage to Jax and the telepath said, *Not a bad comparison. But Caris is the one who is lost. I need something to bring her back to herself. You're the something.*

Why didn't you warn me? Jax asked, cuddling the warm body in his arms closer, rubbing his lips against the pulse in her neck, reassuring himself that her heart still beat, that she still lived.

We tried. But did you really want to hear that Caris can't face crowds unless I walk at her side? Sage's disbelief traveled over their connection and then he glowed with self-satisfaction. *There you are, baby, all nice and warm…*

Jax could feel the memories, that link he had been searching for. Somehow Caris had buried it deep between them and Sage had uncovered it, bringing it to the surface, making Jax's heart race, his teeth ache, his entire body tense with need. *Ease back, lover-boy. She needs the heart and the soul, not the dick,* Sage quipped as he withdrew.

Jax focused his gleaming, angry eyes on Sage, and snarled, "I care very little for your words, your sarcasm…your…*shiel, veca semylyeca?* Heavens, what is this?"

Sage was glowing.

Lowering his hands, Sage cupped Caris' face in his palms and whispered, "Come back, baby. The pain isn't waiting for you this time, I swear. Jax won't let it come back. I won't let it come back. Open yourself up, Caris."

Jax dropped his eyes to Caris' face. No change.

And Sage was still glowing.

"Can she choose to not come back?" he asked.

"Yes," Sage whispered, rubbing his thumbs in slow, gentle circles. "Talk to her, vampire. Call your lover back to you."

Sage settled down on his heels, his lids drooping as he reached out to his best friend with his heart. And Jax, he lowered his lips to her ear and started to croon softly to her, whispering, "My love, my lover, come back to me, come back."

Caris had finally gotten away from that hideous mind-tearing pain. She was safe, warm, and it was blissfully dark and quiet here. Behind Sage's shield. She knew that. The darkness wasn't real. She knew that as well. Sage was protecting her again, as he had always done.

And there were voices…part of her knew they were calling to her.

The other part just wanted to cling to the dark, where she was safe, cuddled, warm. Sage wouldn't make her come out. She knew that, as she cuddled closer to the source of warmth, wrapping herself in his presence as another one pushed ever closer. He'd keep her here, forever, protective, coddling, teasing her once she decided to let him in…

But there was another presence pushing at the edges of the dark, just beyond the barrier of Sage's shield. A different kind of love, every bit as protective, possessive, full of yearning, full of pain…

No! she thought, whimpering and fleeing back into the dark, away from the shield, damning her own curiosity. She could feel Sage's weariness, feel him urging her to relax, to let this other person come in.

Warily, she lowered her own shields to Sage, letting him inside before slamming them up, shutting everything out before she could grasp the pain that hovered at the edges of her mind.

Safe, he crooned. *I'll keep you safe...I've never lied to you, Caris. Come on, babe. He needs you, loves you.*

Caris opened her eyes and blinked, spinning an image in her mind and throwing her and Sage into a dreamscape. When the misty stars dancing in front of her eyes cleared, she found herself crouching on the floor, hugging her knees to her chest, her hair spilling around her shoulders, down her back as she lifted her gaze from the floor to look into Sage's eyes as he knelt in front of her.

She flung herself into his arms, sobbing, thankful to have something tangible to hold onto, even if it was just a dream image. "Sage, I couldn't handle it. I thought maybe this time..."

"Honey, don't," Sage murmured, pressing his lips to her brow. "Don't. You were fine, until the girl. Children are your weakness, you can't help that. And if I'd been there, or if Jax had listened—"

Jax...a strangled sob choked her and she pressed her face against his chest.

"Babe, you gotta let him in. He needs you. He can lead you back to us. I can keep the pain away while you find your way back with him, but I can't do both." Sage pulled away just a little, cupping her face in his hands. "You don't want to stay here."

"It's safer here," Caris whispered raggedly, locking her fingers around his strong wrists, feeling the steady beat of his pulse under her fingers.

"Safer? Yeah, safer. And you can stay, if you need to. If you really need it. But you'll never feel anything real again, no love, no joy, no humor. Never know any laughter again, never see another sunset, never hold a baby, or ride your horses across the land your parents left you," Sage murmured, combing his fingers through her hair, his hazel eyes dark with understanding. "You'll never know if we win, when we win. And we will. We have to. There's so much you'll never know, babe. Is that worth it?"

"Win what?" she demanded. "They kill more of us, all the time. People hate us. How can we win against that?"

"By showing them that we aren't what they think," Sage whispered. "By not giving in. Don't give in, Caris. Come on, Sugar. You've got so many people who love you, need you. Don't give in to the madness of the world. They have taken too many of us already. Don't let them take you, too."

Caris fell against his chest and with a tortured sob, she collapsed the last of her shields.

That overwhelming, powerful presence that hovered just outside her mind coalesced into a shimmering dark blue mist as she stared, frightened, hating herself for her fear, hating Sage for making her listen, the world…

And Jax. He was why she was here, lost inside herself again.

The mist solidified and he stepped out of it, staring around at the dreamscape, confused, his eyes half wild until they locked on her, cuddled against Sage's chest. The intensity in his eyes frightened her. Such emotion, too much! But before she could burrow more snugly against

Sage, he lowered his head and whispered, "He loves you…"

And then Sage was gone, pulling himself out of her mind with a simple thought, leaving Caris rocking back and forth, staring at the ground as she waited for Jax to approach.

Run away run away run away…

By the Blood, Jax thought freezing in mid-step. He wasn't sure of where he was, some surreal plane, one that existed only in Caris' mind, he was certain, but as Sage winked out of existence, leaving him alone with Caris, Jax suddenly felt adrift.

This was no woman he knew.

Lost, frightened, scared as a wild animal…a hot bolt of need streaked through him and Jax lashed it down. Circling around her, he gave himself time to watch, to wait. She never looked up, never acknowledged him. Oh, she knew he was there. She just didn't want to face him, see him, touch him…

Reality existed just beyond him and she couldn't stand the thought of it, he suspected. *Boil my sorry flesh in the suns*, he wished angrily. Why in the hell hadn't he listened?

And why hadn't she pushed harder?

"Damn it all," he rasped, shaking his head and striding across the distance that separated them. She was here. This was Caris. She wasn't in that broken, empty-eyed body back in the mortal plane. She had fled to this place within herself and he had to bring her back out or die trying.

Dropping to his knees in front of her, he caught her arms before she could try to scoot away, just as she was realizing he had moved. She jerked away wildly, her eyes wheeling around, glitteringly jewel-bright with tears. "Caris, beloved…"

A strangled sob ripped out of her throat.

"Do not!" Bringing her against his chest, Jax threaded the fingers of one hand through her golden-amber hair, forcing her to look up at him. "You cannot want to stay here, alone for all of your life."

"Better…than going back…having to do what you expect," she said, her voice harsh and broken, ragged. "I can't fight this war the way you want. I have to do it my way."

Jax felt his heart crumble. She was frightened of him, that he would force her back into what had led her here. "What kind of heartless bastard do you think I am?"

"Not heartless. Just one who doesn't understand what I am," she said tiredly, her head hanging low, hair tangling around her face, hiding her from him.

"And what is that, beloved?"

"Weak," she said softly. "Too weak."

"No." Shaking his head, gently arching her face up, he pressed his lips to hers and said, "Not weak at all. You needed something special, that I didn't know. Beautiful, exotic, warm, sensitive—not weak. Come back, Caris, come back to me. Forgive me for not understanding, for not listening. Though I'm tempted to turn that sweet tail of yours pink for not making me understand."

Caris shook her head. "I don't want to go back, it's so much more painful there."

"And loneliness isn't painful?" he asked, forcing his fear down inside. Sage wouldn't allow him to force her out. She had to come willingly. At the outer edges of his mind, he could feel the other man's presence, a protective cloak that kept all interfering emotions away from Caris as she dealt with her own turmoil. Seething jealousy mingled with gratitude at their bond. Without it, perhaps Caris wouldn't have survived in this world.

But he had to handle her being so close to another man. Even if it was all friendship. It wasn't even the sex that truly bothered him, it was the soul-deep understanding, one he had lacked, until now.

"Loneliness is so very painful, Caris. Heartbreak is painful, what you suffer now must be beyond imagining, but that wouldn't have happened if I had listened, if you had made me. But loneliness, from now until your heart beats no more, stretched out endlessly as you wander this empty plane, no true beauty, no true laughter, no true life…that is loneliness, that is true emptiness. You have truly lived now. Can you go to such a meaningless existence?"

"Yes," she hissed, trying to pull out of his arms. "I want meaningless, if it means safety."

Jax narrowed his eyes and rasped, "Then something to remember as you exist here alone and safe." Arching her neck up, he slanted his mouth across hers, thrusting his tongue past the barrier of her teeth, sliding his free hand up to cup her breast, rolling the nipple between his thumb and forefinger and laughing when she pulled away, trying to bite him.

He nipped her lower lip and ducked his head, raking his teeth along the graceful, pale line of her neck and whispering, "Will you miss this? The feel of my body pressed to yours? Me moving inside you? How it feels when I bring you to climax as the taste of your sweet blood rolls across my tongue like the finest of wines?"

He felt her tremble in his arms as he shifted, sliding his hand down to cup her sex, pressing the heel of his hand against the soft pad of her pussy, the moisture seeping through her pants and panties to dampen his palm as he nipped her lip. "I'll miss it and I'll yearn for you every day, as I care for the empty shell I forced you into. And I'll miss you, my mate, the other half of my soul. The woman I have searched for unknowingly, for years on end. I'll hate myself, knowing I destroyed you.

"Come back to me," he urged, taking her mouth again, cupping her hips and pulling her against him, lifting her so that she cradled his aching cock in the soft cleft of her covered thighs.

Come back to me, he whispered into her mind.

Come back.

Caris shuddered under the hot touch of his hands, the furious joy that raced through her treacherous heart as he rocked his heated length against her, and the agony inside her soul as he whispered the very things that tormented her.

And the last of her resistance dissolved without her even knowing it, as he ate at her mouth greedily. Groaning, she turned more fully toward him, opening her mouth under his and wrapping her arms around him.

"Caris..."

"Thank God..."

"Call Morgan..."

The sound of voices around her was the only thing that let her know her dreamscape had fallen apart. Sage was still shielding her against the onslaught of emotions as she slid back inside her body, aligning her soul with her physical self, leaving behind the safe, secure place where she didn't have to feel. Jax pulled his mouth from hers and stared down into her eyes, his fangs fully descended, his eyes glowing and half-mad with desire, relief, and need.

And love, something so real, so pure, she could feel it inside her heart even with Sage blocking the emotions.

Jax couldn't carry her to bed right away.

Well, he did. That was the first thing Kelly snapped as she strode into the room, her eyes dark with worry, her face pale and tight with strain. But he couldn't strip Caris' sweet body naked and love her until they both collapsed from it. Yet.

Kelly cupped Caris' face in her hands, shaking her head. "I could have killed Morgan. I told him what a damn idiot he was, what they did. Sage didn't go into as much detail as he should have. Morgan didn't truly understand, but he does now. Our fearless leader won't ever ask this again. He finally understands, as much as his male brain will let him."

"The bloody fool would dare ask?" Jax growled, his eyes gleaming, slightly red with rage.

"He will. At some point, she'll be needed. But she has to do it on her terms, her way. Nobody else's way," Kelly murmured. "I think Morgan…finally understood. With a little help."

Caris chuckled weakly. "Kelly, what did you do?"

"Nothing he didn't need to have done, sweetie. In fact, Sage laid the groundwork," she said with a conspiratorial wink. "All I did was finish the work. Now he has an inkling of what it's like to be on the receiving end of too many unfocused, unchanneled, blind emotions."

Caris sighed and closed her eyes. "You two are bad."

Kelly grinned cheekily. "My brother taught me well."

But now, finally, they were alone. Turning his hungry eyes her way, Jax shed his clothes in short, quick motions as he stared at her with stark, naked desire. "I need to feel you against me, naked, as I sink my cock inside you. I need to feel you around me, tight, wet, warm, alive, as you come."

Caris' breathing became ragged as she met his eyes. "I'm exhausted, Jax…"

"You do not need to do anything but lie there, let me have you, and take me," he purred as he stalked closer. Grasping the blankets Kelly had so lovingly tucked around her and jerking them aside, he revealed that slim golden body, clad in a pair of silky white panties and thin white top. Curling his hand into the barrier of the panties, he tore them aside. Sliding his hands under the bottom edge of the strappy shirt, he eyed the dark circles of her nipples beneath and mused, "So pretty…" He pushed it higher, revealing the toned, gleaming flesh, her heaving ribcage as she gasped for air, the bottom, full round curve of her breasts, and the tight pucker of her rosy pink nipples.

Stripping her free of the shirt, he lowered his mouth to take one of the beguiling nipples, suckling deep and rolling his eyes upward to meet her gaze. Bringing his knee up, he pressed it against the smooth, bare lips of her sex, groaning in desperate hunger as her cream slicked against him.

"I want to taste you," he whispered, kissing his way down the line of her torso, pushing her thighs wide and piercing her folds, groaning as the tangy, heady taste rolled over his tongue. The scent of her need filled his head, of her life, of…life.

She was ripe, ready for a child…could they? Would she want it? Savagely, he jerked away. "You're fertile," he hissed.

"…huh…"

She blinked, gasping for air and reaching for him, rocking her hips upward and whimpering low in her throat.

"You are fertile. I do not even know if I could place life inside that sweet little belly of yours, but it is possible. Would you risk it?" he hissed, tossing his streaming coppery hair back and glaring at her.

Her eyes widened. Deep longing flashed in her eyes. "Come back to me," she whispered, reaching up to him. "Yes…I'd risk it. Haven't I proven I'd risk everything for you?"

With a hungry growl, he covered her, driving deep with one long, sure thrust, covering her mouth with his as he buried himself inside her to the core. The hot, tight walls of her sheath closed around him like a greedy, silky fist. Arching his back, he pulled out and pushed back in, shuddering as the walls clenched and worked around him. Her nipples drew into tight, hard beads and Jax lowered his head, drawing one into his mouth and suckling deep, humming in appreciation as it made her sob and tighten around him.

Caris' eyes started to flutter closed and he whispered, "No. Keep them open. I want to see you, you to see me. Feel this…" and he surged back inside her, rolling his hips and caressing the buried bed of nerves by the mouth of her fertile womb. His balls drew tight against him and chills raced down his spine.

Not yet…

"Feel this," he purred again, lowering himself so that the soft pillow of her breasts flattened under the hard wall of his chest and he could feel the smooth, curved lines of her body as she moved under him. Greedy, soft moans fell from her lips, and her heart pounded against his.

"I love you," she breathed against his lips.

"Oh, beloved. I yearn for you, adore you, love you," he rasped as she started to come in long rhythmic pulses around his driving cock, her sharp, eager cry echoing in his ears as he started to pump her full of his seed. "Adore you...love you..."

Long moments later, he lifted his head and studied her pale face. Her eyes were still open, although she desperately needed to be resting. "Will you forgive me?" he asked softly, cupping her cheek. "I did not know."

Her lids lowered.

Jax felt stark terror build within him as her eyes evaded his. "Caris, I am so sorry, beloved," he whispered, lowering his mouth to hers. "So sorry. Don't close me out, please. I beg you."

Beg...he would beg again. He would plead, anything she wanted, so long as she didn't pull away from him.

A quiet sigh filled the air. "You don't need to beg, Jax. It hurt, what happened. I can't just push that away. But I could have made you understand, if I had pushed harder." Her eyes were distant and unseeing as he watched her.

"Why did you not?"

One slim shoulder lifted in a shrug and she responded, "Maybe I wanted to make you suffer. You don't understand, even the memory of what happened in the past is almost as painful as if you had sliced me open. And you kept pushing."

Her voice trembled a little and her eyes finally met his. "I think I wanted you to see — actually see — so it would hurt you too much to even think of doing that to me again," she said quietly.

"It worked," he growled, catching her face in his hands and kissing her roughly. "I don't ever want to see you step foot off of this land again, never go around another person as long as you live, so long as that keeps you safe and whole."

"That might be a bit extreme," she murmured, her lips curling up in a smile.

"Are you going to forgive me?" he demanded, pressing a bruising kiss to her mouth. "I cannot live without you, and I cannot live with the cold creature you have become. It hurts me to even look at you and see those empty eyes."

She smiled, sadly. "I forgive you, Jax," Caris said on a sigh. "My pride led me here as surely as anything you did."

"I love you," he said urgently against her neck. Nuzzling the patch of skin where the vein throbbed beguilingly. "I adore you, and I'll kill to keep you safe. Die to keep to you safe."

"Hmmm. I won't ask either. Just love me," she whispered, lifting up and pressing her lips to the crown of his head. "Just love me."

"Ah… my beautiful dreamer, I can do nothing else," he swore as he slid his knee between hers and worked his aching sex inside the swollen tissues of her pussy.

Time spun away as he loved her, lowering his head to feed from her, rocking his hips against her slowly, taking his time to bring her to climax, reveling in the moans and sobs that fell from her lips.

"My beautiful dreamer," he whispered as she started to come. "All mine. Forever."

"Hmmm, my vampire," she murmured as he collapsed against her a long time later. "Ya know, I think the best thing I ever did was dream of my vampire just a little while ago."

Damn it.

This could be a problem.

He was here to protect her, to warn her, to teach her. And considering she had been living with her head in the sand for more than twenty years, that wasn't going to be an easy task. Being attracted to her was going to make it even more difficult—but if he felt the wolf inside him, felt the call of hers...

There was no if.

She was an Inherent born, if not yet changed. And he was a very gifted Inherent, a Hunter to the Council, and one of the few who had a touch of witchery through his mother's side of the family. He was a powerful witch, and that was how he had found her, but he suspected what he had in his veins was nothing compared to what lay untapped inside the woman in front of him.

Jillian had more than a touch.

Her mother had gifted her with such powerful witchcraft that it was amazing the earth didn't tremble as she walked. That a powerful, evil, dark seeker hadn't found her and tried to subjugate her.

Amazing that he had found her first, and was thinking that their powers and magicks wouldn't call to the other?

There was no if.

Stop it, Ben. We don't even know if she has the abilities, he told himself, shaking his head. He could smell something other than human on her, but that didn't mean she was an Inherent like her father had been. And the magick he smelled on her didn't mean she was a witch like her mother had been. She had gone more than a decade past the time when she should have first shifted. And no witch could ignore the call of magick for more than twenty years. Just because some old witch saw her thirty years ago, years before her birth, and said she would come in time to help fight some unknown war…

Visions were always subject to change. And maybe it was another Inherent.

Hell, if she was a witch, an Inherent, she would have changed when that werewolf attacked her five years ago. If she had…and if she had still been sentenced to jail…

And damn it, it had been Agnes Milcher who'd had the vision. Agnes…

Even as solitary as Benjamin was, he had heard of her. Her name evoked the same feeling that the vampire Malachi's did.

Shaking his head, he muttered, "Stop creating trouble where there is none. Wait and see what happens. See if she truly is gifted before you start planning."

He was also trying to fool himself.

Oh, she was a witch all right.

And an Inherent.

But somehow she had kept herself from changing.

Somehow she had suppressed her magick.

Or somebody had done it for her. From beyond the grave, perhaps?

For years.

She was the daughter of Carrick Wallace, one of Declan O'Reilly's father's right hand men. He and Adrienne had been murdered and their young daughter had gone missing twenty-three years ago. After Declan had walked away so many years before, the pack had reformed, restructured, and had executed the rogues.

They had searched high and low for Shadoe Wallace, the young babe mourned by so many.

And that child was Jillian, the woman who had fought off two rogue shape-shifters, a werewolf and an Inherent, and killed one of them.

She had done time in jail for protecting herself when she should have been coddled and praised, loved, adored, worshipped — shit, it made him furious just thinking of it. If he had found her just a little sooner, none of it would have happened.

Hell, maybe he was wrong. Maybe she wasn't an Inherent in truth. How could she have resisted the call of the moon, the call of the hunt, the magick of feeling the wolf's call for more than a decade?

She may not be a true shape-shifter, but she was more than human now.

He just had to figure out exactly what she was.

And soon. Before their enemies arrived.

* * * * *

"Ms. Morgan."

She went stiff.

Jillian knew that deep, almost growling voice. That voice had fueled a couple of very *interesting* dreams during the long, empty years in jail.

Benjamin Cross. Slowly she turned and met a pair of golden eyes across a distance of a few feet. She hadn't even considered that he would try approaching her. And now she realized just how foolish that had been. His persistence had known no bounds, so why had she suddenly expected that to change?

"I've no desire to speak with you, Mr. Cross. I do not give interviews," she said firmly, stifling the urge to stare as she gazed upon the man who had been calling her on a monthly basis for five years.

The phone calls had started within a month of her incarceration. At first, he'd just offered to come in and speak with her about her ordeal. Then he'd offered to 'interview' her for a book deal. Then he'd offered to interview her regarding her books. Although how he had discovered *that* piece of knowledge she didn't know. Then he'd just started calling to pester her.

Politely. Always politely.

But the phone calls never stopped.

A year into her sentence, letters had started coming, along with research books on magick and shape-shifters, and ghosts. The majority of her better books had in fact come from the man staring at her with those mesmerizing golden eyes.

Holy hell. It was a damn good thing she hadn't known what he looked like, otherwise she just might have given in to those interviews. Just for writer's curiosity, mind you…but *damn.*

His dark brown hair fell into his eyes in loose waves and he absently brushed it back with a lean, tanned hand, cocking his head and studying her intently. "You didn't really think I would just up and leave you alone, did you?" he asked, curiously.

She had the odd impression of a pup staring at her with his ears pricked. Or a wolf…shaking her head, she focused on a point just beyond his shoulder and said,

"Actually I hadn't thought of it." Her eyes cut back to him as she added, "Or you."

"Ouch," he said mildly, those amazing brown eyes dancing with humor.

Of course, if she had known what he looked like...*oh, that would have been torture in there,* she thought helplessly.

Underneath the green chamois shirt he wore, there was a ribbed undershirt that stretched across his wide chest, his skin gleaming gold, muscles clearly evident beneath the clinging fabric. Worn jeans clung to his lean hips and long, muscled thighs as Jillian cursed her peripheral vision and forced herself to meet his eyes.

They looked...hot, hungry... A smell assaulted her senses, the smell of lust and the primal need to mate. Though how she could place such a name to that hot musky scent, she didn't know. Any more than she could figure out how she could smell it so clearly.

Hell, his eyes—gleaming, glowing...the striations in his eyes were starting to swirl and shift...

Unbeknownst to her, a soft whimper escaped her as she stared hypnotized into those eyes. She had seen eyes like that once upon a time and fear arced through her. A gasp fell from her lips and she retreated, her eyes wide and unblinking on his face.

And as she watched, the look left his eyes, his lids drooped, the odd tension seemed to leave him, and a gentle smile curved his mouth, the full lower lip curving just slightly. "I'm no threat to *you,* Jillian Morgan," he said softly, his voice intense. "To those who threaten you, I bring death—slow and painful—but I am no threat to you, ever."

He turned and left.

About the author:

Shiloh was born in Kentucky and has been reading avidly since she was six. At twelve, she discovered how much fun it was to write when she took a book that didn't end the way she had wanted it to and rewrote the ending. She's been writing ever since.

Shiloh now lives in southern Indiana with her husband and two children. Between her job, her two adorable and demanding children, and equally adorable and demanding husband, she crams writing in between studying and reading and sleeps when time allows.

Shiloh Walker welcomes mail from readers. You can write to her c/o Ellora's Cave Publishing at 1337 Commerce Drive, Suite 13, Stow OH 44224.

Why an electronic book?

We live in the Information Age—an exciting time in the history of human civilization in which technology rules supreme and continues to progress in leaps and bounds every minute of every hour of every day. For a multitude of reasons, more and more avid literary fans are opting to purchase e-books instead of paperbacks. The question to those not yet initiated to the world of electronic reading is simply: *why?*

1. *Price.* An electronic title at Ellora's Cave Publishing runs anywhere from 40-75% less than the cover price of the <u>exact same title</u> in paperback format. Why? Cold mathematics. It is less expensive to publish an e-book than it is to publish a paperback, so the savings are passed along to the consumer.

2. *Space.* Running out of room to house your paperback books? That is one worry you will never have with electronic novels. For a low one-time cost, you can purchase a handheld computer designed specifically for e-reading purposes. Many e-readers are larger than the average handheld, giving you plenty of screen room. Better yet, hundreds of titles can be stored within your new library—a single microchip. (Please note that Ellora's Cave does not endorse any specific brands. You can check our website at www.ellorascave.com for customer recommendations we make available to new consumers.)

3. *Mobility.* Because your new library now consists of only a microchip, your entire cache of books can be taken with you wherever you go.

4. *Personal preferences are accounted for.* Are the words you are currently reading too small? Too large? Too...**ANNOYING**? Paperback books cannot be modified according to personal preferences, but e-books can.

5. *Innovation.* The way you read a book is not the only advancement the Information Age has gifted the literary community with. There is also the factor of what you can read. Ellora's Cave Publishing will be introducing a new line of interactive titles that are available in e-book format only.

6. *Instant gratification.* Is it the middle of the night and all the bookstores are closed? Are you tired of waiting days—sometimes weeks—for online and offline bookstores to ship the novels you bought? Ellora's Cave Publishing sells instantaneous downloads 24 hours a day, 7 days a week, 365 days a year. Our e-book delivery system is 100% automated, meaning your order is filled as soon as you pay for it.

Those are a few of the top reasons why electronic novels are displacing paperbacks for many an avid reader. As always, Ellora's Cave Publishing welcomes your questions and comments. We invite you to email us at service@ellorascave.com or write to us directly at: 1337 Commerce Drive, Suite 13, Stow OH 44224.

Discover for yourself why readers can't get enough of the multiple award-winning publisher Ellora's Cave. Whether you prefer e-books or paperbacks, be sure to visit EC on the web at www.ellorascave.com for an erotic reading experience that will leave you breathless.